Royal Flush

Scott Bartlett

Mirth Publishing
St. John's

ROYAL FLUSH

This novel is a work of fiction. All of the characters, places and events are fictitious. Any resemblance to actual persons, locales, or events is entirely coincidental.

© Scott Bartlett 2011

Library and Archives Canada Cataloguing in Publication

Bartlett, Scott
Royal Flush / Scott Bartlett ; illustrations by Susan Jarvis.

ISBN 978-0-9812867-0-9

I. Title

PS8603.A784R69 2009   C813'.6   C2009-905103-6

For Mom, Dad, and Danielle

The King
of
Hearts

The glass chimes on the front door tinkled and the Kingdom's sole glassblower raised his head. "Now who?" he said, and peeped out from his cramped back room, only to hastily withdraw.

"The gods have mercy," he whispered.

He squeezed his eyes shut, but the image remained imprinted on his eyelids. Standing in the front room, staring imperiously down his nose at a glass unicorn, was none other than His Royal Highness, the King.

During his long career the glassblower had come to know well the sound of priceless glass artwork breaking. It was this sound that now penetrated the curtain separating both rooms. The glassblower winced. The unicorn had been his finest work.

The reason for his distress had little to do with destroyed masterpieces, however, or with the import of visiting royalty. It had everything to do with fear for his life. Though the glassblower never attended one, it was well known that public executions were held frequently in the Royal Square. They were so frequent, in fact, that the majority of those executed couldn't possibly be guilty of anything—except perhaps of displeasing the King in some insubstantial way.

"Isn't anyone back there?" the King said. "You mustn't keep me waiting! I'm terribly busy, and my dungeon is full, and I have only one way of dealing with this kind of insolence!"

Clenching his teeth to halt their incriminating chatter, the glassblower stepped out, glad for the wooden counter between himself and the King. The craftsman prudently averted his gaze from the pile of broken unicorn at the monarch's feet.

"Good morning, Your Majesty," he grunted through clamped teeth. "What a pleasure to have you in my humble shop." Again he winced. He was a terrible liar.

The King took no notice. "I want to commission a piece of your work," he said.

The glassblower noted the King's composure, or rather his lack thereof. The royal garments were unwashed and rumpled, and a royal stench made the glassblower wrinkle his nose. The King was a mess.

Nevertheless, he came with a business proposition, and so the glassblower adopted his most professional manner. "For whom will I be crafting this piece, Your Majesty?"

"The biggest harlot in my entire Kingdom."

The glassblower hesitated.

"And what shape shall it take?"

"A heart," the King said, his voice wavering. "I want it shaped like a heart, and I want it to be extremely delicate."

"Delicate, sire?"

"Yes, you overblown peasant. Delicate." The King paused. "I want it to break in her hands."

The glassblower cleared his throat. "Am I right in thinking, then, Your Majesty, that you want a piece of artwork that will break, but only when it is held by a certain maiden?"

"That's correct."

The glassblower swallowed. What the King asked was virtually impossible. Stalling for time, he said, "I take it this woman has wronged you, Your Highness?"

"I take it you wish to be flayed?"

"Forgive my intrusion, sire," the glassblower said quickly, "but why not simply imprison her?"

"Because I love her," said the King, and started to cry. "I'll be back for it in two days." He left the shop, sobbing.

The glassblower gazed vacantly as the entrance bell announced the monarch's departure. It might as well have tolled the craftsman's funeral.

The King's assignment was unfeasible, and so there remained only two courses of action. The glassblower could stay, dutifully working to fill the King's order, and ultimately failing—and probably losing his head in the process—or he could leave, forever abandoning the store his family had managed for generations.

Thirty minutes saw the glassblower barrelling north with only a horse, his tools and a few pieces of carefully wrapped work.

3 days before

"I love you!" exclaimed the King. "You are the sun around which my world orbits! Nay, the sun pales next to your scintillating beauty! You are the rose whose splendour a name does no justice! You are the object to my subject! The adjective to my noun! You—"

"Are you finished yet?" said the woman to whom he spoke, yawning.

15 days before that (arguably the beginning)

The King looked down upon his home and tried to decide if it was a palace or a castle.

The very fact he looked *down* at it betrayed the edifice's strangeness. It occupied the trough of a valley, and was surrounded by the houses and shops of peasants, many of whom could glance down upon the King whenever they wished.

There was even a nearby hill upon which his home might have been built. It was currently occupied by shepherds and their herds, but it would only have been a matter of paying them off—or exiling them, convenience permitting—and the structure might have dominated the countryside.

Instead, the royal architects had seen fit to construct it upon the lowest point in the land. One architect was kind enough to inform the King the enormous building was actually partly below sea level, which accounted for the frequent flooding during the rainy season.

The previous castle—or palace, or what have you—had also been constructed at the very bottom of the valley, which might explain the ease the invaders enjoyed when they infiltrated and burned it to the ground. Since they took nothing, and departed immediately after setting the royal domicile ablaze, no reason could be found for the invasion, except perhaps to criticize the Kingdom's architectural integrity. The monarch at the time—the present King's predecessor—stubbornly ordered the new castle/palace built in exactly the same spot.

After surviving an invasion, a fire and a wagonload of bad publicity, the former King perished from eating a bit of uncooked meat at the banquet celebrating his newly constructed abode.

After the previous monarch's demise, the present King leaped up to join the struggle for the throne—to find he was the only one standing. No one else wanted the job. Even the former monarch's sons expressed no interest, instead choosing to take up horseshoeing in a village ten leagues to the west. The King became the King by default.

He shrugged off the depression his hybrid-home never failed to elicit and returned to his waiting steed. It bleated loudly. You might be quick to point out horses don't bleat—they neigh—but this horse *did* bleat, by simple virtue of not actually being a horse. It was a goat. All the horses in the royal stables had contracted colic, forcing the King to use this slightly less conventional mode of transportation.

Presently, it began to rain. The King grimaced, and pulled his cloak tighter.

The goat bleated again. He had given the beast a name, however it is rather a vulgar one, and therefore must not be recorded here.

An oversized saddle rested on the animal's back, and had a propensity for shifting about, often depositing its rider onto the ground. It was in this the King now attempted to sit. Cautiously he circled the goat, murmuring calming words, which were drowned out by the creature's protests. He tried placing his foot in the stirrup, but the goat shied away. His frustration grew, until finally he flung himself awkwardly onto its back, causing the cantankerous beast to take off with the King half in and half out of the rain-slick seat. Petrified by the goat's acceleration, he held this precarious position for dear life.

As they barreled through the muddy streets, the King clutching the saddle horn as the saddle shifted wildly about, some peasants shouted advice on goat riding from the safe dryness of their doorways.

"See if you can grab its horn!" shouted one.

"Kick it in its flanks!" suggested another.

Whether their ideas would have helped or hindered, the King dismissed them without thought. He suffered from an unfortunate excess of education which, much like a microwavable dinner left in till it crisps, had rendered him beyond repair. He respected only opinions that originated within his own cranium, and since those of the peasants hadn't, the King D.Litt. Ph.D. D.Agr. D.Arch. Th.D. Ed.D. D.B.A. D.D. D.A. D.M.A. D.Mus. D.C.L. Dr.P.H. Psy.D. LL.D. P.L. ignored them.

It is only appropriate that next the goat charged through the campus of Kingdom University, knocking over academics as it went and causing them to scream articulately at the King.

The goat exited the campus, the King still miraculously astride. He noticed it had brought him near his home, albeit in a roundabout way. Indeed, the royal moat was at the end of the very street along which they now galloped. He speculated briefly about whether the beast's lunacy would allow it to stop.

The goat *did* stop. The King, however, didn't. He continued moving through the air, until at last his flight ended with a large splash. Floundering, saturated and sputtering, the King decided it must be a castle, after all. Only castles had moats.

"Your Highness!" said a high-pitched, barely masculine voice. "Whatever are you doing down there? You're going to be late!"

Of the many unfortunate things the King had inherited from his predecessor, the man who now addressed him was perhaps the worst. He was slim, unimpressive, and sometimes mistaken for a woman. He possessed an uncanny knack for turning up during the King's darkest moods.

"Being late," the King answered, treading water, "implies previous knowledge of an engagement. I had none."

"But sire, I *did* tell you! I told you this morning I'd hired a bard for your entertainment!"

"Oh. Well, it also implies caring. And I don't."

The man was the King's advisor, and unlike most royal advisors—who conducted themselves according to hidden agendas—he actually seemed to care about how the Kingdom was run. This made him insufferable.

"Sire," the advisor said as he helped the King out, "you really must stop swimming in the moat. Don't you know it's nearly winter?" He smiled. "It's a good thing I advised against the man-eating alligators, now isn't it?"

The King glowered. Shivering, he tried with futility to wring out his garments.

His mood enjoyed no improvement as they traveled the castle's near-empty corridors. The King found it difficult to find anyone willing to work for him, and had grown adept at tricking unwitting applicants into signing contracts. That was how he'd acquired his stable master.

"Do you suppose my subjects dislike me?" the King asked his advisor.

"Er, of course not, sire. I suspect they merely feel unworthy of working for you."

The King digested this. "Now I remember why I keep you around."

The hallways were filled with tapestries and statues: remnants of the former King's reign. The present King hadn't altered much, except to smash a few pieces of artwork on his bad days. He wasn't much of an interior decorator, and he was yet to hire any masons for the castle's upkeep. As a result, it was falling apart.

The bard waited in the throne room, tapping his dulcimer impatiently. At the King's entrance he launched into his narrative, accompanied by an up-tempo melody.

> *"There once was a King who everything owned:*
> *Or at the least, everything that mattered."*

The King smiled.

> *"Everything, that is, except for a wife."*

The King frowned.

> *"It might be argued that the gracious King*
> *Would eventually wed a lady*
> *Who in the Kingdom lived. Logically,*
> *Since he owned the Kingdom, he owned a wife*
> *As well. He owned them all, technically."*

The King began to redden.

"That is not the point," the bard said quickly,
having noted the King's discontentment.
"The point is that the King wasn't married.
Without a mate, he could produce no heir,
And without an heir, who would make the rules?
One had to have rules, else folks misbehaved.
Wouldn't you, were there no one to make rules?"

The King turned to his advisor. "I don't *care* about rules!" he screamed. The bard tactfully began a musical interlude. "People can do as they bloody well please!"

"Sire, it's only a story!" the advisor squeaked.

A purple vein asserted itself on the King's forehead. "I'm not a dunce—I know a thinly veiled allegory when I hear one. I *was* schooled at Kingdom University, you know!"

"At least let him finish!"

The bard began the second half of his ballad.

"For years the King ruled wisely and fairly,"
he sang, nearly choking on the untruth,
"With the help of his friend, the advisor.
With time, however, the noble monarch
Passed away, leaving no heir to make rules,
And do other kingly—"

Now crimson, the King was grinding his teeth audibly. The bard hurried on, abandoning pentameter.

"With the King's death, the Kingdom descended into a dark, lawless period, emerging from it only after adopting that nightmarish bane of all rulers—democracy."

On this grisly note, the bard stuffed his dulcimer into its case and fled, having both noted the King's foul mood and recalled the monarch's fondness for executions.

The King rounded on his advisor. He hissed: "You've taken your last liberty, vermin." He began to advance, and the advisor began backing up.

"But sire!" he said in what he hoped was a calming tone. "As King, it is your duty to marry! The Kingdom needs an heir to the throne. Do you remember what happened the last time it lacked one?"

The King halted momentarily, furrowing his brow. "Yes!" he growled. "I became King!" He rolled up his sleeves and continued his approach.

The advisor, in retreating, bumped into the throne and fell into it. Realizing where he sat, he nearly wept in horror, but could not get up without kneeing his liege in the face.

The King glared up at him. "Mark my words: I—will—not—marry!"

"Yes, but sire!"

"Yes, but sire!" the King mimicked, his voice cracking. "Yes, but sire! Is that all you know how to say, you bureaucratic twit? But sire, *rules,* sire! Bugger your blasted rules! Did you hear that? Bugger!"

A shocked silence ensued.

"But sire!"

The vein pulsing on the King's forehead seemed in danger of exploding. Finally he threw up his hands, wheeled about and marched out of the room.

The advisor leaped up from the throne as if scalded.

7 flagons of ale later

"Barman! 'Nother flagon."

The tavern keeper came over and eyed the King dubiously. "Your Highness, you've already had several."

"Mmph. Know what else I've had? Several men executed. Bring me another bloody flagon."

The tavern keeper shrugged and went to get the King's drink.

The King continued to stare into his empty mug. He was a champion drinker. Of course, he got a lot of practice. It wasn't easy being King, and every bartender in the Kingdom knew it.

One day, shortly after his coronation, the King had announced that the gods endorsed his rule, and that he bore the mandate of heaven. He much preferred this to the truth: that he was King because no one else wanted to be.

A month or so after this declaration, a group of farmers marched into his throne room. "This year's harvest is lousy," they said. "It's your fault."

"*Me?*" said the King. "Why blame me?" He glanced nervously around the room, his gaze settling on a guard. "Why not him?"

The guard looked up. He blinked.

"We blame you," the farmers said again. "For the harvest, and for the hurricane last Tuesday."

"That's ridiculous. You can't blame me for the weather."

One of the farmers dared to position himself within inches of the King's face. "We sure can," he said. "You said yourself you rule by divine right. If there's something wrong with the harvest, or with the weather, then it must mean you've done something to anger the gods."

The King stared at the farmer, his mouth working wordlessly. He couldn't believe it. In consolidating his rule, he'd somehow given his subjects licence to criticize him for absolutely anything that went wrong.

A *clink* jolted him from his gloomy reverie. The tavern keeper had returned with his drink. The King began downing it immediately.

The tavern in which he sat obeyed the three D's: dark, dingy and dilapidated. He preferred such bars over other, nicer establishments, because he was less likely to encounter young nobles with bright ideas about how the Kingdom should be run. He couldn't decide who he disliked more: farmers who condemned him or busybody nobles who tried to help.

Thinking about nobles and farmers only made him more depressed. It seemed somebody was always storming his throne room with a complaint or a suggestion. He never had any peace. He sighed.

"You look like you've had a rough day," observed the two women who appeared beside him.

"You don't know the half of it," the King muttered. He turned to look at them. "Are you twins?"

The two women eyed him askance. "Er, there's only one of me."

"Ah. Sorry. I'm very drunk."

"I can see that. In fact, I was just now given to wondering what would occasion such a conspicuous display of alcoholism."

"In short, I'm having marriage shoved down m'throat." The King hiccupped.

"I know what that's like. I've lost count of how many guys have tried to swindle me into wedlock. So, who's this unshakable woman?"

"It's a man, actually."

The woman's brow furrowed. "I'm sorry, I don't think I heard you correctly. Did you say a *man* is trying to talk you into marrying?"

"Aye, a colleague of mine. He says it's for the best."

"I see. I suppose there's no point in continuing this conversation, then." The woman bade him farewell, and left the bar.

The King stared into his drink in consternation. He knew something had gone awry, but he had no idea what. It would have consoled him to know he wouldn't remember any of this in the morning.

"Where did I go wrong?" he wondered aloud.

The tavern keeper spoke without looking up. "She thinks you're gay, sire."

The King's drink exited his mouth. "She thinks I'm *what?*" he said. "Not that there's anything wrong with that sort of thing, of course." He began to stammer. "Nothing at all. It's just that—I don't—I've never—"

The King grimaced. "Get me another flagon."

the next morning, 5 hours before the King's hangover subsides

"'Let other men play at other things,'" the advisor said as they rode out onto the enormous polo field. "'The King of Games is still the Game of Kings.'"

"I like that," said the King. It served to distract him from his throbbing head, which the driving rain and cutting wind were doing nothing to improve. "Did you come up with it?"

"I read it on a stone tablet."

The King and his advisor squared off in the center of the field. The King had commissioned the construction of the polo field under the guise of promoting public recreation. Then he forbid anybody else from using it.

"Outline the terms once more," the King commanded.

"Very well. If you win, I promise never to mention the prospect of matrimony again." For some reason, the advisor's words made the King think of last night. "If I win, however, you must agree to one date with a maiden of my choosing."

"Fair enough," the King said. "Let's decide handicaps."

One of the primary reasons the King had yet to dismiss his advisor from service was that he alone matched the King's ability in polo. This was not to say the King was in any sense of the word *good*—quite the opposite, in fact. Both men were so inept that serious players refused to play with them, even under threat of death. And so, the King's abiding infatuation with the pastime granted the advisor superb job security.

The game of polo involved horses, mallets, a ball, and a lot of needlessly complicated rules. The King wasn't completely familiar with all of them, but his favourite part was the declaration of handicaps that preceded the game. It had become a popular strategy with the King and his advisor to arrive in as miserable a condition as possible. This morning, the King expected to gain a staggering lead.

"You start," the advisor said. "And remember, the rain doesn't count."

"I'm extremely hung over."

"Okay, that's one point for you. My horse has colic. That's worth two."

"Very well. I'm riding a goat."

The advisor contemplated the King's mount for several seconds. "Hmm, okay, that's worth two goals."

The King's brow furrowed. "Do you jest? Perhaps you misheard me—I'm riding a *goat*."

The advisor sighed. "Fine, I'll give it three. Now I'm two, you're four."

"That's more like it."

"I've got the flu."

"Just nasal?"

"Nasal, chest *and* head."

"Okay," the King said with reluctance. "You're up to three."

"Any more for you?"

"Of course. I'm royalty, and unused to physical exertion. You're three; I'm six."

"*Six?*"

"Okay, five. Next."

The advisor cast about for another one. Finally he said, "I have a lot on my mind."

"You have a lot on your *mind?* Are you seriously venturing that as a handicap?"

"Um, yes."

"And how many is that worth?"

"Two or three."

"Two or *three?* Well in that case, I can never get a moment's peace because my insufferable advisor pesters me incessantly! That's worth at least seven!"

The advisor drew himself up indignantly. "Is that so? Well I get nine goals because I'm an underpaid, underappreciated professional whose employer is a tyrannical jerk with the maturity of a six-year-old girl!"

The King and his advisor glowered across their mounts, panting.

"What's the score now?" the advisor snapped.

"I can't remember," the King growled.

"Let's just play."

They wheeled their mounts about viciously, each player riding fifty yards away from the ball, which sat in the very middle.

"Are you ready?" the advisor shouted.

"What a redundant question!"

"Oh, of course—I'd forgotten! You never are!"

And the game commenced, the opponents barrelling across the pitch with abandon.

Halfway through its charge, the King's goat suddenly tucked its head into its chest, horns aimed directly at the opposing horse. This had two significant effects: the advisor hastily turned his mount, fleeing in the opposite direction, and the King grinned widely and wickedly.

"That's right! Run, you self-important fleabag! Advise your way out of this one!"

The goat reached centerfield, and the King's mallet connected with the ball. It traveled a pitiful five yards. Thankful the advisor's back was turned, he chased after it. This time his mallet struck home with a robust *smack,* and the red orb followed a pleasingly broad parabola. The King let forth a triumphant roar.

Desperate to escape the goat's horns, the advisor veered toward the left side of the field. The goat also steered left. The King's heart sank.

"No!" the King cried. "Bad, stupid, animal! Go toward the ball!"

Above the rushing wind and galloping hooves, the advisor could be heard laughing wildly.

The advisor's strategy developed from there. He took to leading the King around the immense field in wide circles, looping around to seize control of the ball. The King tugged the goat's horns and kicked it in its flanks, but to no avail. The mindless beast was content to chase the opposing steed indefinitely. By the second seven-minute chukker—polo's rough equivalent to a period—the advisor had scored nine times.

When the game ended with a score of seventeen to zero, the advisor dismounted fluidly, giving his horse a hearty slap on the rump. The animal took off into the downpour. Doggedly, dim-wittedly, the goat followed.

"Good game, Your Majesty!" the advisor shouted as the King hurtled past. "You owe me a date!"

Impotently furious, the King could only cling to his wayward steed as it carried him far into the wilderness.

a long walk back later

Wet, tired and hungry, the King stormed into the throne room and fell into the royal perch. The walk back had given him a lot of time to reflect. He'd mostly reflected on how angry he was.

"Bring the cretin!" he yelled.

The guards knew exactly whom he meant.

"Hello, Your Majesty," the advisor said timidly as he skulked into the room.

"Give me one reason I shouldn't hang you from the castle's highest parapet."

"You're afraid of heights."

The King glared. "I've been walking the whole afternoon in the rain—that horse of yours ran for an entire hour!"

"Oh? And then what?"

"It turned and kicked my goat in the head!"

"Well, how is it?"

"Dead, I hope! I left it in a ditch."

The guards opted not to inform the King both horse and goat had returned around noon. They often failed to inform him of things, as a sort of general precaution.

The advisor spoke. "Sire, I believe we had an agreement."

"I hoped you'd forgotten."

"Far from it. Your date awaits you in the dining chamber. Dinner is almost ready."

The King turned white. "You set the date for *tonight?* But I look terrible! I haven't shaved in days! What will we talk about?"

The advisor gently guided the King out of his throne, making soothing sounds.

"I need a bath!" the King said. "I'm much more charming when I've had a bath."

"Nonsense. Just play up the fact that you're obscenely wealthy. Women go crazy for that sort of thing."

"Are you sure that's the best way to cultivate a loving relationship?"

The advisor ignored him.

They arrived at the cavernous dining chamber and found a striking young maiden sitting at one end of the lengthy table.

"She's half my age," the King whispered, shocked.

"I know. Not bad, eh?" In a louder voice the advisor intoned, "Your Highness, meet your date for tonight. I'll leave you two to introduce each other." He gave the King a sly wink.

The King settled down in the chair opposite the beautiful maiden. The table seemed to stretch for miles, but he still felt they were too close. An awkward silence settled over the dining chamber.

"My name is Georgianna," the woman announced at length.

"Is it really?" said the King. "I'm so sorry."

The woman made a face. The King sensed he had begun poorly. He reached for something else to say.

"Er, so, what does Georgianna mean? I bet it has a really grand meaning."

"It means 'gracious farmer'."

"Ah," said the King. "Well, it could be worse. It could mean 'ill-mannered farmer'."

A brittle quiet resumed. "So," said the King, and the syllable hung in the air, punctuating their conversational constipation.

"I'm a pretty rich guy."

ten minutes later

When the advisor arrived with the first course, he found the King slumped in his seat. The opposite chair was empty.

"Where's Georgianna?"

The King gave a start, but quickly schooled his face to innocence. "It's funny you should ask, actually. I—"

"Where is she, Your Highness?"

"I had her thrown in the dungeon."

"You *what?*"

"Had her thrown in the dungeon."

The advisor set down the food—roast duckling, lovingly sautéed, served with freshly picked ginger root and asparagus—and sat in Georgianna's empty chair. His chin trembled. He began to weep.

"It's not as if she isn't comfortable!" the King said. "I gave her my best cell—had to release the nobleman I arrested last week! You know how I dislike releasing prisoners without good reason."

"Why," the advisor said through a sheen of tears, "did you throw your date in the dungeon? Do you think that's the right way to treat a lady?"

"It's certainly one way," said the King. "What else was I supposed to do? She wouldn't say anything! She was making me uneasy!"

"Small talk, Your Majesty. It's called small talk."

For a time, they said nothing.

"Do you have any idea how long it took to prepare this meal?" the advisor abruptly wailed.

The King eyed the elaborate platter. "A long time, it would seem."

"The asparagus and ginger root are from my garden! I plucked the duck myself!"

"Well, there's no sense in letting good food go to waste. Let's eat."

The advisor stared at the King, his jaw set. He sighed. "Fine."

Georgianna was soon forgotten.

"This sauce is exquisite," said the King, his voice muffled. "It complements the, um, the asparagus rather nicely."

"You have no idea what you're talking about, do you?"

"Not really, no."

"The sauce is crushed plum. And the asparagus is meant to cleanse the pallet."

"Jolly good. Look, you should really drop this marriage business. It isn't going anywhere. I'm just not the marrying type."

"Of course you are," the advisor mumbled through a mouthful of food. "You just need to find the right girl, that's all."

"But who says I've got to marry?" The King paused to tear off a chunk of duck. "Is there some kind of universal rule?"

"It's just what you do. Everyone has to pay income tax, and everyone has to marry. Brandy?" he asked, proffering a bottle.

"Yes, please." The advisor stood up and started around the table. The King continued: "But *I* don't have to pay income tax. I'm the King."

"That *is* a bloody good point," the advisor said, returning to his seat.

The King held up his chalice.

"More brandy."

The advisor blinked. "But I just—"

"It's gone."

The advisor stood up again.

"Anyway," the King said, "what woman in her right mind could ever come to love someone like me? I'm a cruel person by nature. Why, last week I drowned an entire bagful of kittens. Just for the hell of it."

"Actually, it's funny how these things work themselves out," the advisor said, walking back to his seat and leaving the brandy bottle next to the King. "I was talking to the owner of those kittens, and as it turns out, they all had terminal prostate cancer. Every last one of them. So from that perspective, you did a noble thing."

"How curious," the King said. "But what about back in August, when I tricked some small children into believing their parents were dead, and that they had to live out the rest of their lives in an abandoned coal mine? Surely there's no justifying something like that."

"As a matter of fact, it's the same sort of thing. Those kids had all contracted a particularly infectious strain of the plague. You probably saved the Kingdom by arranging their exile. The parents were grateful for the holiday, at any rate."

"Hmm. And the puppies I had beaten last month?"

"Mongrels, all. Terrible mongrels. Given to tearing through the marketplace making an awful racket."

"The innocent man I hanged for sport?"

"Innocence is subjective."

"The village I burned to the ground?"

The advisor paused for thought. "No one can prove you did that."

"Incredible!" the King said. "I really am a swell fellow!"

"A beacon," the advisor managed around a mouthful of roast duck, "of moral light."

"But still not suited to marriage."

The advisor's face fell. "Why not?"

"Listen, I know what marriage does to a man, okay? It makes him a mindless drone. A mindless, *sober* drone," he added, viewing the latter adjective as the most significant. "How many happy husbands are you acquainted with?"

The advisor opened his mouth to respond, but the King cut him off. "Don't answer that. If any man claims to enjoy marriage, it's because his wife is in the room."

Once more the advisor sat silently for a long time, looking at the King. Finally he stood up, his expression set. "Sire, this Kingdom deserves an heir, whether you see it or not. Since you refuse to cooperate, there remains only one option." He walked toward the door.

"What?" the King said. "Are you going to go on strike?" He chuckled.

The advisor reached the door and turned around. "No," he said. "I'm going to the Kingdom Crier."

And with that ominous pronouncement, he departed.

several stunned seconds later

The King sat, dumbstruck, with an asparagus stalk hanging out of his mouth.

"He wouldn't."

He ran to the door and out into the corridor. All that remained of the advisor was the patter of his feet, rapidly receding in the direction of the stables.

"He would!" the King cried, and sprinted down the hallway after the traitor.

The Kingdom Crier was the most respectable newspaper in the Kingdom, but only because it had run all the other newspapers into the ground. The Crier busied itself by printing fantastical stories about prominent citizens of the Kingdom, flirting only occasionally with fact. The baker, for instance, purportedly used sawdust in his flour, and the butcher, who was also a swordsman, had been accused several times of duelling and cutting meat with the same blade.

The King was a frequent target. Enraged at an article that speculated about his taste in underpants—to a frighteningly accurate degree—the King once ordered the entire staff of the Kingdom Crier executed. The newspaper, however, merely responded with an article bearing the headline, "CRAZED MONARCH ORDERS THE ENTIRE STAFF OF THE KINGDOM CRIER EXECUTED". Hundreds of angry peasants picketed his drawbridge for days, abating only when the King rescinded the order. Despite its transparent lies, the Crier's readership included practically the entire Kingdom.

He reached the door leading to the stables and tried to open it. The doorknob came off in his hand. "Blast!" He would have to run around and enter through the outside.

Outside, it was raining.

He finally stumbled in, dripping. Several seconds passed before he could muster the breath to address his stable master, who sat on a nearby stool eating a sandwich. The King, as mentioned previously, was embarrassingly unused to physical exertion.

"Did my advisor pass this way?"

"Aye, he did, Your Majesty. He took off on horse just moments before your coming." The stable master frowned. "Is that an asparagus stalk on your collar?"

The King ignored him. "Get me a horse. A fast one."

"Can't do that, sire. They're all colicky."

"What about the advisor's horse?"

"It's got colic, too."

"Then why did you let him go?"

"He have me this sandwich."

"Where did he get a—?" The King shook his head. "Get me a horse or I'll have you hanged!"

"Would that void my contract, then?"

The King balled his hands into fists. "Curse you! Haven't you anything at all I can ride?"

The stable master jerked his thumb at a shadowy stall in the corner. "Got this goat."

The King looked in the direction his stable master was pointing. He stared at the goat in disbelief. "*You*," he said under his breath. The goat bleated challengingly.

"All right," he said finally. "Saddle it."

The stable master did so, and between the two of them they managed to get the animal into the stable yard. It was still raining.

Looking up, the King spotted his advisor on a distant street, pummelling his horse for more speed. He'd nearly reached the Kingdom Crier. The King leaped onto the goat's back and yelled, "Quick! After that horse!"

The goat remained motionless.

"Come on!" yelled the King, booting the beast in the ribs. "Just like on the polo field! *Charge!*"

The goat bleated, and began to nibble at a patch of grass.

"Confounded animal!" The King itched to send someone to the headsman.

Disaster was averted when the stable master delivered a valiant boot to the animal's rump. It took off, bleating indignantly.

Whether by divine intervention, generosity on the goat's part or plot convenience, the goat brought him directly to the offices of the Kingdom Crier. Or rather, the animal rocketed past the offices of the Kingdom Crier, and at that moment the King launched himself from its back. The impact knocked the wind from his lungs. The goat carried on running, though the King had a feeling he hadn't seen the last of it.

He hurried into the lobby, gasping for air. The receptionist—an attractive, efficiently-dressed young maiden—greeted him with a patronizing smile.

"Did a short, womanly man come through here recently?" the King asked her.

"Your advisor is seeing the Editor, Your Majesty."

"Well I want to see him too. Which way?"

"I'm afraid I can't allow it. I'm afraid I have specific orders to deny you access beyond the lobby."

"Aren't you also afraid I might have you executed?"

"I'm afraid I'm *not* afraid of any threats you may utter, as they've been proven quite ineffective."

The King smouldered.

A funny whooshing noise came from behind the receptionist, and she turned to extract a small, rolled-up scroll from a tube that ran up the wall and through the ceiling.

Having read the message, she once again turned her condescending smile on the King. In her eyes, he could see his intelligence being reduced to that of a child. A particularly delayed child.

"It appears you've been granted special entry to the Editor's office for today only. Take the stairs on your left."

The King trudged away from the desk, resentful he did so only with permission.

The Editor, Duke Edward, worked on the seventh of eight floors, or so an embossed plaque told the King. "Why not the eighth?" he said. "Does he expect anyone to believe he possesses even a shred of humility?"

"The eighth floor is the Observatory," said a passing journalist.

"Hmph," the King said, certain their telescopes were pointed forever downward, and never up. He started up the stairs.

The seventh floor consisted of a single cavernous hallway, with the double doors of the Editor's Office situated at the very end. As he traversed its length, the King thought about all the worthless, fraudulent smut that had passed through the doors ahead. He felt soiled.

He knocked on the giant oaken doors, and was made to wait an entire minute before someone opened them. It was his advisor.

"Why, Your Majesty!" he cried, more horrified than welcoming.

The King punched him in the face, sending him staggering back into the office. Then he too advanced into the room, looking to repeat the act two or three times.

"Now, Your Highness," scolded the man who sat behind an imposing desk, also of oak. "We'll have none of that here. I have a loaded crossbow in my desk, and I'm loath to take it out—conversation seems to simply dry up whenever I do. If I see it as necessary, however, I will. Please beat your employees on your own time."

The King concentrated the full force of his rage into making a hideous face.

The man winced. "Your countenance is repellent enough as it is. Don't do it the injustice of contorting it further."

The King clenched his fists.

"You do know who I am?" the man said. "Of course you do. I'm the one whose intimacy with the contents of your laundry basket rivals your own. I'm the one who knows all too well about the nighttorch you keep in your room while you sleep—that's the subject of our next big exposé, by the way." The King grimaced. "I," said the man, pausing for effect, "am Duke Edward, Editor in Chief of the Kingdom Crier."

"You're a filthy swine," the King spat.

Edward smiled. "That, too."

The two men tried to stare each other down, one angry, the other amused.

"Who made you a duke, anyway?" the King said.

"The previous King, in exchange for our discretion concerning his affair with the Lady Beatrice. Who, as you are probably aware, was married to the ruler of a powerful neighbouring Kingdom."

"But you did print that! Directly following the invasion!"

Duke Edward shrugged. "Times change, and so do agreements. Speaking of agreements, your advisor and I have made quite a swell one! Haven't we, old chap?"

The advisor was attempting to disappear behind a potted fern. He moaned.

"Of course we have!" Edward cried, treating the advisor's dread like hearty confirmation. "I invited you up, Your Majesty, because I felt it would be a shame for you to miss it. Your advisor has been kind enough to divulge a piece of fascinating information, and for our part, the Kingdom Crier is going to print it. It's the least we can do. Wouldn't you say, sire?"

The King's fury prevented him from saying much of anything.

"I can see the headlines already!" the Editor went on. "'SELFISH RULER REJECTS REPRODUCTION, SEALING KINGDOM'S CHAOTIC FATE!' Or maybe: 'FROM A SELECTION OF DE-MOCRACY, SOCIALISM OR FASCISM, OUR KING CHOOSES ANARCHY!' I think that has a certain ring to it. What do you think? You're looking rather pale, if you don't mind my saying, Your Highness."

"You'll pay," the King managed.

"Oh, please," said Edward. "I think we all know where the real power lies in this Kingdom."

The King sputtered. "I'm the one with the executioner!"

"Ah, but Your Majesty, you've overlooked a simple truth: the pen is mightier than the guillotine."

"If you're so powerful," the King said, "then why don't you take the throne for yourself?"

"I don't want it!" said Edward, sounding genuinely surprised. "No one does—that's why you have it." He smiled. "You may leave, now."

The King had a better idea. It involved his clenched hands, and Duke Edward's neck. He stepped forward.

As promised, Edward produced a loaded crossbow. A grim still-ness descended on the office.

"I told you this thing kills conversation," the Editor said. "Now, both of you: leave."

an issue of the Kingdom Crier later

The King plodded dejectedly through the marketplace. All around him, hawkers endorsed their wares loudly enough to drown out the customers' cries of indignation. The goods were of poor quality, for the most part, and overpriced. Nevertheless, the King purchased a parrot in a desperate attempt to improve his mood.

"Get married, you boob!" it squawked.

The King returned its vacant gaze with one of his own. "What?" he said.

22

The parrot bit his nose and flew away.

"Sorry about that, sire," said the vendor from whom he had bought the bird. "Guess I forgot to clip its wings. Gave good advice though, don't you think?"

The King spied a copy of the Kingdom Crier under the hawker's stool, and felt his ire rise. He was so depressed, however, he lacked even the energy to have the man hanged.

"Boil your head," he said instead, and moved on.

As he walked, he looked imploringly at the sky. He wondered if the gods were paying attention.

It began to rain.

A giggling couple passed him, running to get out of the wet. They were clearly in love. The King made a rude gesture at them.

The exchange of goods wasn't slowed much by the weather. The various vendors and storeowners couldn't afford to close shop, except in extreme conditions. A living was hard enough to come by without closing for a little drizzle.

A pauper approached him through the rain, brimming with happy vigour.

"Beautiful morning, Your Majesty!" he said as he fell in step with the King. "Don't you agree?"

"I don't wish to share my opinion on the matter."

"Ah, can't be put in words, you say!"

"Not the words you're using."

The peasant grinned, apparently impermeable to the King's negativity. "Pardon me, sire, but I've got something of a proposition for you."

The King radiated an utter lack of interest.

"I was reading the Kingdom Crier, and—"

"Stop right there."

"Pardon?"

"I said you can stop right there. I don't want to hear any more."

"Right, so I was reading it, and couldn't help but think—"

"Shut up!"

"—got this sister, see, and—"

"Close your lowbred mouth!"

"—real pretty little thing, right? Anyhow, I figured, you being hard up for a wife and all—"

"I'll have you caned!"

"—I figured you two should get all matrimonial and whatnot!"

The peasant ended by patting the King companionably on the back.

"Agh!" the King screeched, backing away and shuddering. "Never, ever lay a hand on the royal person again!"

Obliviously, the peasant withdrew a wallet from his grimy pocket and began to show the King drawings of a gap-toothed maiden of around fifty. "There she is, Your Majesty. Real beauty, wot? Here," he said, thrusting the drawings into the King's hands. "You can have 'em!"

The King dropped the papers as he would a pile of hot coals. He stared at his hands. "Now I have to get these amputated!"

The peasant's expression finally lost its glow. "Now, Your Highness, there's no need to start talk about getting things surgically removed."

The King looked wildly around the marketplace for somewhere to wash himself. "Help! I need to bathe! I'm unclean!"

"T'was only a gift, sire. I only wanted to show you my sister."

"Bring me soap! Paint remover! Anything! I've been touched by a commoner!" He looked at the peasant again. "A particularly dirty commoner!"

"She's a pretty one, that's all, and *I* can't marry her, so I thought I might as well do you a favour and introduce you."

By now the King was tugging madly at his clothes and hair. Duke Edward, his advisor and this peasant had all conspired to rob him of his sanity. They had succeeded.

"So I'll just be getting her, and you two can get on with the married life. Be back in two shakes of a—"

"Excuse me, is anything the matter?"

The King ceased his raving; the peasant, his mindless babble. They both looked appraisingly at the woman who approached them.

Suddenly, the King gazed upward in disbelief. It had stopped raining.

"I didn't think it possible," the peasant said, "but she's even prettier than my sis. I suppose there's no point in my fetching her now. She'd look like a dandelion next to this azalea." He slumped off, dejected.

24

"Good riddance," said the King.

"I hope you don't mind my asking," the newcomer said, "but aren't you the one on the newspaper's front cover? The one everyone's saying should get married? Aren't you..."

"The King?"

"I thought you were gay."

"Er, you did?" The King frowned. "Is it the shirt?" He looked down accusingly at his attire. "I knew I should've worn something else."

"No, no. You told me."

"I did?"

"Yes. You were drunk."

"I often am."

"In a bar. The other night."

Hazed memories floated to the surface of the King's consciousness, bursting like bubbles of stale air. As he strained to remember, he looked at the woman and felt a strange, fluttering sensation. He couldn't name it just yet, but its eventual classification would lead directly to his advisor's demise.

"I *do* remember," the King said. "And I don't quite know how to say this, but—"

"I got completely the wrong impression."

"Precisely. Not that there's anything wrong with..."

"...that sort of thing," the woman finished for him.

The King smiled awkwardly, his face being quite unused to the exercise.

The woman grinned as well, somewhat more competently. "I'm glad to finally have you placed, then. I'll see you around."

The King's face remained in its novel configuration as the woman departed. He finally realized what he'd felt as he looked at his new acquaintance. It was love.

10 years later

"You know," said the former King from a ditch, to no one in particular, "I think that girl really messed me up."

He took another prolonged draught from his pocket flask.

For days, the King's thoughts had been occupied with one thing only.

"Is anything the matter?" his advisor asked him earlier that morning.

"Not at all. Why do you ask?"

"You haven't ordered anyone beaten, imprisoned or hanged for going on seventy-two hours."

Ever since he parted ways with the maiden in the marketplace she had been on his mind. He thought about her while asleep. He thought about her while awake. He thought about her while he brushed his teeth in the morning, when he was someplace in between.

The only time he didn't think about her was when he thought about all the other maidens living in the Kingdom, and how they didn't quite measure up to her.

That he lacked even her name should have reconciled him with his senses. But it only increased her mysterious allure.

The King was in love.

On this cool autumn afternoon the King was mooning about his throne room. His roaming gaze settled upon a pile of dusty manuscripts, and somehow, his fevered brain drawing a ridiculously complex web of interconnectedness, they reminded him of her. A light breeze entered through the open window, and it prompted him to wonder what his goddess might be named. His gut told him 'Daphne', but in his heart, 'Diana' felt right.

His advisor entered the room. He still sported a black eye from the day at the Kingdom Crier.

The advisor cared deeply for the Kingdom's welfare—far more than the King, Duke Edward or anyone else realized. He is probably the most wholesome person who appears in this tale—indeed, as will have become evident by its end, he is one of the few who deserve to be termed 'decent', or even 'civilized'. In the face of unemployment, injury and execution, he is still willing to stand fast for what he believes to be right.

It is only fair we honour him in this way, given that by the end of the scene he will be dead.

"Sire?" the advisor began timidly. "Are we on speaking terms?"

"What?" the King said, still deep within his romantic reverie. "Oh. Sure."

"You're not still angry I went to Duke Edward?"

"Duke who?"

The advisor decided not to press the matter. He steeled himself with a deep breath, and continued: "Sire, I brought someone for you to meet."

On cue, a young woman of breathtaking splendour walked into the throne room. The immaculate presentation of her gleaming brown tresses suggested she'd spent half her life combing them, and the other half staying out of sunlight. She curtsied primly.

"Her name is Elsie," the advisor said, his voice gathering strength. "She is the daughter of a well-to-do saddle maker. She is educated, polite, and beautiful." Elsie blushed. "She is also modest. She is in possession of all her teeth, and her name is perfectly regular."

The King began to show signs of life. He looked upon Elsie. The advisor carried on:

"I ask only one thing, Your Highness. One very small thing. I would like you to speak with Elsie, for ten minutes. That's all I ask— one brief conversation. I don't want you to ignore her. I don't want you to have her thrown in the dungeon. I want you to talk. And in the unlikely event you prove at all compatible, I would like you to consider courting her."

The King stared at the advisor through the haze that had obscured his vision for the past three days. "I can't."

His liege's reply made it very difficult for the advisor not to strike him. He spoke in clipped tones: "*Why—in—Hades—not?*"

"Because I love another."

At these four words the advisor fainted dead away, falling sideways and dashing his skull against the floor and scattering brains across the marble.

Elsie's mouth worked for a full five seconds, eventually releasing a scream worthy of the most prolific banshee. Her shriek seemed to go on indefinitely, until finally she turned to the King with a helpless, horrified expression.

"What are you so worked up about?" the monarch said. "He was a nuisance, anyhow."

Outside, thunder rumbled. It began to rain heavily.

a worryingly short time later

"'HE WAS A NUISANCE, ANYHOW': HIS MAJESTY'S FINAL FAREWELL TO HIS MOST FAITHFUL ALLY."

The King's hands shook as he read the incriminating headline.

"Bugger," he said.

In truth, his worry was not so much concerned with the storm of public outcry sure to follow, but with what his new love might think.

"I should do something to fix this," he said.

He paced the throne room, wishing he had someone to discuss the matter with. "Let's see. My colleague died unexpectedly, and I'm about to get lynched by the entire Kingdom. As well, my love life stands to suffer. What *does* one do in a situation like this?"

He mulled it over for half the morning, pacing the throne room and yelling at anyone who entered. He considered the dilemma from every angle. At length, something flickered inside his cranium.

"Brilliant!" he said, wondering at his own ingenuity. "I'll hold a funeral!"

the following afternoon

The crowd of peasants gathered in the Royal Square muttered angrily as the King took the podium, trying his best to look sombre. From this vantage point, he could see many of them carried dangerous-looking projectiles. He concentrated on not allowing his legs to give way.

The King had assumed the funeral itself would be sufficient to appease his disgruntled subjects, however he could see he sorely miscalculated. If he cherished his life—and, all things considered, he did—he would have to deliver a bloody good eulogy. Luckily, his scribes had spent the entire night writing one. He had yet to read it himself, but they assured him it was their finest work. He smoothed it out on the podium.

A drop of water smote the paper in its dead center, causing the ink to trickle and marring an entire paragraph. The King looked up, unable to accept what was happening.

28

It began to rain in earnest, and the eulogy was quickly rendered illegible. The King cursed. He would have sworn the sky was clear mere minutes before. "Why is it always raining in this blasted Kingdom?"

He cast his gaze over the assembled throng. They looked back at him impatiently, many of them stroking their assorted weaponry. The King swallowed. He would have to improvise.

He racked his brains for a compliment to pay his deceased associate. There had to be something the King had liked about him.

"My advisor," he began, "was a terrible polo player."

The crowd booed loudly. The King ducked, barely dodging a battleaxe that hurtled toward him from one of the front rows.

Frantic, he cast about for something else to say. "His level-headed advice is the reason many of you have avoided the headsman for so long."

The crowd entered a frenzied rage, seething forward as one. The King squeaked. They intended, it seemed, to tear him apart, piece by royal piece.

"Wait!" he shouted, holding up both hands. "Wait! I'm not finished!"

The crowd paused impatiently.

"During his brief life," he rushed on, "the advisor's foresight often spared me tremendous hardship—much like the wickedly sharp and pointy hardship I'm facing this very moment."

The crowd gave a reluctant chuckle.

"Once, he saved me from becoming the meal of man-eating alligators, by persuading me not to include them in the royal moat. Which," he added, "I recently had the misfortune of falling into."

This time, those assembled laughed outright. The King could hardly believe it. He was winning the crowd over. Gaining confidence, he said, "Of course, the man was completely incompetent when it came to mixing a drink."

The crowd growled.

"I guess what I really mean!" he shouted above the mounting tumult. Gradually, it subsided. "I guess what I really mean to say is my advisor was the only man in the Kingdom who remained by my side without having to be bribed, swindled or threatened." He hesitated. "In fact, he remained *despite* being bribed, swindled and threatened."

The crowd murmured appreciatively. The King noted with shock that many of them were moved to tears. They began to set down their various projectiles.

"The advisor was my dearest friend," he concluded, placing his hand over his heart, "and for that reason I will miss him dearly."

The peasants gave a deafening cheer, clapping and pumping fists in the air. The King took this opportunity to quietly remove himself from the center of attention. He used his sleeve to wipe a trickle of sweat from his brow.

He walked through the castle town's empty streets in utter disbelief. Not only had he completely renounced all morality, but he had done so in full public view. And somehow he emerged from the ordeal unscathed.

He rubbed his eye and was surprised to see his fingers came away moist. He grunted.

A familiar rhythmic patter reached his ears. He frowned. When had he heard that sound before? From whence did it come?

Suddenly an intense pain exploded in his buttocks, and he flew forward several feet, landing unceremoniously on his face. A shadow leaped over him, momentarily obscuring the pale sun, and continued its charge down the road in the direction of the castle.

The King looked up. He cursed fiercely. It was the blasted goat.

a joyous discovery later

The King clutched the perfumed letter to his chest, unwilling to let himself consider for a second it might be real.

Five minutes prior he had barged into the stables, red-faced and respiring rapidly. "Where is that infernal beast?" he demanded.

The stable master looked up from his stool, where he sat reading the Kingdom Crier. "What infernal beast would that be, Your Majesty?"

"That…that *goat.*"

"Oh. He's in the corner stall, there. You got a message, by the way."

The King strode toward the stall door and gave it a mighty jerk. It wouldn't budge. The goat bleated defiantly.

"Oh, you filthy animal," the King snarled. "When I get this door open, I'm going to thrash you to within an inch of your mangy life."

"A woman came and delivered it. Real pretty like. Wore a veil, but you could see she's real pretty. Told me to give you the letter soon as possible."

The King was attempting to grab the goat's horn. "C'mere! I'll tear it off and make a candleholder!"

"You're lucky to get mail, Your Highness. I never get mail."

The King ceased his fruitless efforts and turned around. "What are you talking about?"

The stable master handed him the letter. As he read it, the King's heartbeat tripled.

Dear Your Majesty,

I hope you do not think me too forward in writing you. I have been thinking about you since last we met. I must admit, our misunderstanding concerning your sexual orientation continues to amuse me.

Have you found a bride yet? I hear they are difficult to come by this time of year. Much easier in the spring—with all the impressionable young maidens lolling about, it hardly requires any effort at all. Or so I've heard.

The main purpose of this letter is to request your companionship tonight. If you accept, please meet me on top of Shepherd's Hill at six. If you decline, then merely remain absent.

I hope to see you soon.

At the bottom of the letter, she had written her name. It was utterly ordinary. It was perfect:

Alice

"Doesn't mess around, this one," observed the stable master, who had been reading over the King's shoulder. "Heck, if you're not going I will, Your Majesty."

Ignoring him, the King savoured the moment. It was hard to conceive only yesterday he hadn't even known Alice's name. Today, he held proof that not only had she thought about him, but she also didn't completely revile his company.

"What time is it?" he said.

The stable master stepped out to study the sun, and returned with an answer. "5:52."

The King's mouth formed a grim line. "Saddle the goat."

a blessedly brief ride later

Darkness descended in inverse proportion to the King's anxiety. He was at least a half hour late. He wanted to kill something, and only refrained from doing the goat in because of its obvious importance to his arrival.

The King's distress clashed with the lazy calm evening brought to the Kingdom's streets. Children were being called in from their play. Street vendors were packing their wares. It made the King wonder what it was like to live without supplicants harassing him, tabloids defaming him and peasants attempting to lynch him.

He attained the summit of Shepherd's Hill as darkness descended. The goat's bleating mingled with that of countless sheep, creating a cacophony that set the King's teeth on edge.

"Good evening, Your Majesty," a soft voice hailed him from his left. The King's heart made a home in his throat. He turned his head to behold Alice, looking even more striking than he remembered. Teasing, she said, "Is this what you call fashionably late?"

"I can be either charming or punctual," the King said. "Never both."

"Care to have a seat? The show is about to start."

The King dismounted, eager to discover what sort of 'show' Alice had in mind. The goat busied itself with chasing sheep about the hilltop.

"I like your mount," Alice said. "Such an abundance of hair."

"And of horn," the King agreed, speaking from experience. He lowered himself gingerly onto the blanket Alice had set out, his rear still sore from his earlier encounter with the beast. "Now, about that show you mentioned…." He regarded her expectantly.

"Look!" she said, pointing to the sky with slender fingers.

He lifted his gaze. This wasn't going as he'd hoped. "And what is it I'm supposed to be looking at?" he asked with more patience than he felt.

"The first stars are being unveiled!"

The King looked at her levelly, his lack of interest clear. "Is that so?"

But Alice only lay back on the blanket, affording her a wider view of the dark panorama. She patted the space beside her.

Suppressing a sigh, the King also reclined on the blanket. He viewed the bright dots with growing disinterest.

More stars appeared. The quiet stretched on. The King shifted awkwardly, fearing their conversation was stunted already. Alice just gazed into the sky.

"Do the stars look the same to a king as they do to a commoner like me?" she asked, turning her head to face him.

"No."

"Why not?"

"Because, unlike you, I have a clear view of both your beauty and the stars. In contrast, the latter cheapens considerably."

Alice laughed. "Do you expect I'll let you kiss me after saying something like that?"

The King frowned. "I don't see why you shouldn't." He thought this an awful reception of the first sincere compliment he had ever delivered.

His sulking was interrupted when Alice drew close and pressed her lips to his.

When at last they drew apart, Alice smiled. "You should call your goat, sire. It's getting late."

"Um, okay."

Calling his goat was an embarrassing affair that involved nearly getting skewered. When he had subdued the animal, he asked Alice how she arrived.

"I walked." She arched an eyebrow. "You're not going to offer me a ride on that shaggy brute, are you?"

"Well...."

Alice winked and stood next to the animal. "I'll walk," she said, but took the King's hand across the goat's backside.

Man, woman and goat made their careful way downward. The sky was in full bloom now, and devoid of clouds. When the King and Alice parted ways at the bottom with a final kiss, he felt ten pounds lighter. He was beginning to think perhaps he had finally found happiness.

Wouldn't *that* have made for a boring story!

after 7 hours of amazing sleep

The King's reign had taught him an unfortunate lesson.

For years, he had presumed himself to be in some way special. And in most respects, this was true—all things considered, he *was* the ruler of a great expanse of terrain.

With matters of the heart, however, truths that otherwise served perfectly well no longer applied. Logic was done away with, along with sense, practicality and consideration for the mental health of all involved.

Being a stranger to the brambles of love, the King's subsequent behaviour acknowledged none of these regrettable facts.

"My, my," the King said to himself when he awoke at five in the morning. "I *am* wonderful. What woman can resist my endearing quirks, my lightning wit, my ox-like build, or my endless riches?" Realizing what he had just said, the King added, "Scratch that last. A guy like me doesn't need riches to woo a wench! Clearly women love me for who I am."

He paused, his brow furrowing. "Or do they?" He remembered what the advisor had said about his 'obscene wealth', and its power to attract women. How could he ever be certain Alice liked him for his personality, and not his pocketbook?

He summoned the royal accountant—a short, mousey man whose default expression seemed to be one of perpetual worry.

"I wish to donate my entire fortune to charity," the King informed him.

The tiny man's expression shifted from worry to near strangulation.

"Er, have you thought about this, sire?"

"Of course!" the King said. "For at least three minutes."

The accountant took to wringing his hands as one would a dishcloth. "Have you considered the benefits of, say, *not* donating your entire fortune to charity?"

"Hmm," the King said. "I suppose that might be nice. Yes, I can see how that might work for certain people. But I don't think it's me."

"Your generosity is admirable, my liege, but I feel I must insist—"

"There is a fine line between *insisting* and *insubordination*. Is that a line you feel up to treading?"

The small man shook his head.

"Excellent. Now get to it."

The accountant trudged away, wondering whether he should off himself before or after fulfilling the King's request.

"Goodness," the King murmured, continuing his soliloquy from where he'd left off. "Shedding one's accrued wealth is rather taxing."

He settled carefully into his throne—mindful of his still-aching bottom—and decided to await the next correspondence from his love. That he was completely certain it would arrive only worsened his shock when it didn't.

what seemed an eternity later

Time passed so slowly he nearly stopped believing in it. The movement of the sun told him two days had passed, but his yearning heart spoke of centuries.

The King couldn't account for Alice's absence. He envisioned countless haunting scenarios. What if Alice was hurt? What if she had been somehow robbed of her faculties for moving, writing and speaking, and therefore was unable to visit him, mail him or order pizza?

What if Alice had assumed she wasn't good enough for the King?

It is one of life's little ironies that the single possibility not considered by the King was the only one that reflected reality.

The King decided to address his dilemma piece by piece:

He loved Alice.

He wished to communicate his love to Alice.

He didn't know where Alice lived.

Well, if he couldn't speak to her directly, then he had to speak to the group of which she was a part. In short, he required a method of delivering a message to the entire Kingdom.

He now teetered on the brink of a solution. He could feel it in his bones.

"I need an airship," he said. "Or a lot of posters, or…"

He stopped. All colour drained from his face.

"…or a newspaper," he said with quiet dread.

And that was how he ended up in the lobby of the Kingdom Crier for the second time in nine days.

thirty minutes later

The King stood up and brushed himself off as his goat charged past the Kingdom Crier, lacking its rider. They had entered a relationship of mutual abuse—the product of which, to the King's amazement, was that he ended up where he wanted to be. The King hadn't quite come to like the goat, but he at least began to enjoy loathing it.

Inside, the same receptionist awaited him with the same condescending leer. "Hello, Your Majesty. I'm afraid you don't have access beyond the lobby today. Or any day hereafter, for that matter."

"I don't need it. I want to place an ad."

The receptionist seemed disappointed. She handed him a scroll. "Here are the prices."

For a fifty-word ad:
Children – 8 pence
Adults – 12 pence
Seniors – 6 pence
The King – 70,000 pounds

The King gaped. "Seventy thousand *pounds?*"

"That's what it says, isn't it?"

"That's more than my castle's worth," he said. He took out his wallet.

It was empty.

"I've been robbed!" Something stirred in his memory. "Oh, wait." His accountant's face materialized in his mind's eye. It regarded him sternly. "Bugger."

He turned back to the receptionist. "Listen, I can't afford that."

The receptionist held her fingers in front of his face and snapped them sharply. The King blinked. "Hey!" she said. "Stop wasting my time! I'm trying to do a crossword." The King looked down, and saw it to be true. The Kingdom Crier had its own crossword. The receptionist continued: "If you don't have the cash, then no transaction will occur, and no ad will be placed. *Capeesh?*"

She returned to her puzzle.

The King stared bleakly at the complex grid.

"But I really need it," he said.

A familiar whooshing noise sounded from behind the receptionist. She extracted the scroll from its tube and read it aloud: "Tell His Majesty if he joins me in my office a deal might be struck. Signed, the Editor."

The King raised his eyebrows. "How does he know I'm here?"

The receptionist heaved a sigh at their sustained dialogue. "He's the editor of a tabloid parading as a newspaper. It's his business to know everything."

The King gave a distracted nod. Squaring his shoulders, he headed for the stairs. To see Alice again, he was prepared to part with anything but his soul. Well, perhaps a portion of it.

"Hey," the receptionist called after him. He turned. "What's a four-letter word for 'incompetent figurehead'?"

seven floors later

"Your Majesty!" Duke Edward said warmly. "You look terrible!"

The King looked down at his dusty, rumpled garments. "Confounded goat."

"Calling me names won't get you what you want, sire. But then, working against your goals *is* in accord with your usual policy."

"What do you want from me?"

"Straight to business, is it, Your Highness? Fair enough. First, I want you to admit I am infinitely more cunning than you are."

"Very well." The King could see no harm in complying within the empty office. "You are—"

"No, no. Sign this." Edward handed him an adorned document. It read,

The illustrious Editor Duke Edward is infinitely more cunning than I am.

The King grimaced. He closed his eyes and autographed it.

Duke Edward snatched the paper back. He picked up an empty frame that had been sitting on his desk and carefully inserted it.

"There," he said, placing the item where it was clearly visible. "I've been waiting a long time to have that—like a bothersome itch you can't quite scratch."

"Is that all? Can I have my ad placed now?"

"Not quite. There is one more thing. A mere trifle."

The King swallowed. "What is it?"

The Editor grinned. He curled his forefinger. "Come closer."

The King bent forward imperceptibly.

"Closer," Duke Edward whispered, delighting in the King's suspense.

Grimacing, the King leaned across the desk.

"I want you," the Editor said, pausing for two full beats, "to put on a woman's dress, and let our artists paint your portrait."

The King drew back. "You want *what?*"

"You," the Editor said, "to put on a woman's dress, and let our artists paint your portrait."

"That's sick."

"Wrong," Duke Edward corrected with emphasis. "It's news."

"I am *not* putting on a woman's dress and makeup just so you can—"

"I never said anything about makeup. But that's a bloody good idea…"

"I won't do it! I refuse!"

"Very well," Edward said, leaning back and folding his hands on the desk. "We have no deal. Please leave."

The King turned to go. He thought of Alice. He stopped. He thought of her slender fingers.

He turned back.

"Okay. I'll do it."

"Splendid," Edward said, leaning forward once more. "There's a changing room to your left. You'll find the dress inside. I'll have someone fetch the makeup."

"I really, really revile you," the King said, and entered the changing room.

"Don't skimp on the eye liner!" Edward barked.

an incredibly long time later

The changing room door creaked open, ever so slightly. The voice of a broken man emerged.

"I can't come out."

"Why ever not, Your Majesty?" Edward asked in a singsong voice. He winked at the others present in his office.

"I don't want to talk about it."

The Editor crept silently toward the door, placing his finger over his lips in a shushing gesture. The others suppressed snickers.

He yanked it open, and the King stumbled out. At least, logically speaking it could only have been the King, since no one else had entered the changing room since the makeup was delivered. But what the gathered painters, reporters and Editor saw when the door opened could only be a very bulky, very masculine woman.

"He did a great job with the lipstick," one artist said.

The King began to sob.

"Stop!" Edward said. "Stop crying! You'll cause your makeup to run!"

The artists set about assembling their easels, and the reporters began scribbling furiously on notepads.

"Stand like this," Duke Edward said, placing one hand on his hip and the other hand on his head. *"Do it!"*

Trembling, the King imitated the pose.

"Get him from every angle," the Editor went on. "Make sure you can see the whole dress. Blast, I should have had him wear heels, too. Can you paint those in?"

For two excruciating hours, the artists reproduced the spectacle that was the King on canvas. As he stood, his arms burning from remaining in the same position for so long, the King remembered every man he ever sent to the gallows. He remembered them, and he envied them.

At long last, the Editor circled the room, inspecting each artist's rendition. "Exquisite," he announced. "Masterful works of art, all. It's almost a pity they're going on the front page of a smut paper."

His attention returned to the King. "You can leave."

"What about my ad?" the King asked, his voice wavering.

"Oh. That." Edward thrust a scrap of paper and coal into the ruler's hands. "Hurry up. I've got a newspaper to print."

The King wrote his message with shaking hands, and handed it over.

The Editor studied it. "Hmm. This will contradict the main article. It'll have to go in the very back."

The King was too downtrodden to argue. "I need my clothes." He started for the changing room.

Edward tried to hold back a creeping, insidious smile, but failed utterly. "Your Majesty?" he said.

The King slowly turned to face the Editor. "Yes?"

"I had them burned."

days later

For the hundredth time, the King perused his copy of the Kingdom Crier. His dead eyes digested the headline listlessly.

'FINALLY COMING CLEAN: THE KING CONFESSES TO DRESSING LIKE A WOMAN, AND BEING PROUD OF IT'.

Slowly, he ran his finger down the text, reading with a stony face. It hardly elicited a reaction anymore.

Earlier today, the King approached Editor Duke Edward with an astonishing revelation.

"His Majesty and I go way back," says Duke Edward. "He's always come to me for advice and guidance, but today he seemed especially distraught."

The Duke goes on to explain how the monarch fell to his knees in the middle of the Editor's Office, weeping.

"I asked him what the matter was, and at first he could hardly speak. I held him until he settled down. That's when he confessed: he enjoys putting on women's clothing."

The kind-hearted Duke shakes his head compassionately as he recalls the incident.

"At first it was in the privacy of his own bedchambers. He told me he used to put on only high heels, or maybe just a bonnet, and study himself in the mirror.

"Eventually, however, the situation…well, to be frank, it got a lot worse. He began wearing full women's attire, as well as makeup. He started frequenting taverns and bars in his new outfits. He became so adept no one could tell the difference—I'm sure you can see that from the pictures. But the King has been a good friend of mine for years, and I knew I had to do my best to help him out."

Duke Edward used an old trick of the trade (he's a jack of many) called reverse psychology. He took a dress and makeup from a chest of old costumes left over from his Thespian days, and made the confused ruler put them on. He gave him a mirror.

"'Look,' I said to him. 'Look at yourself. Are you proud of this? Is this the way you want to live your life?' And the King just looked at me and answered, 'Yes, Edward, I think it is.' I knew then he was beyond any help I could give."

Following the Duke's valiant effort to lend a hand, the King walked all the way back to the castle, still wearing the womanly outfit. He was sighted several times along the way.

"It was bloody revolting," one infuriated man states. "And to think I nearly let him marry my sister…"

…continued on pages 3, 7, 10, 13, 14, 21, 27 and 30.

The King turned to the very last page of the newspaper. Situated in the bottom left corner, printed in almost microscopic font, was his short ad:

Attn: Alice. I have strong feelings for you, and I miss you very much. Please write me another letter or visit me at the castle. I don't know where you live.

I've been looking at the stars every night since we last met. You were right about them. They're magnificent.

Several days had passed since the ad was printed. This issue of the Crier had already been read by everyone in the Kingdom.

Alice wasn't coming.

that night

The King sent for his accountant to see about regaining his fortune, only to find he had quit. It made a certain sort of sense—by definition, accountants require something to count.

He discovered a modest sum he had squirreled away in his mattress. It was just enough to drink until he got alcohol poisoning and died. He smiled.

Purposefully, the King plunged into the rain in search of the seediest, dingiest inn he could find. He passed several that were either one or the other, but tonight his standards of seediness and dinginess were very high. "Hey, Your Pervertedness!" shouted a peasant from a second story window. "Where's your tutu?"

The King responded with a rude gesture.

A building loomed in front of him. Half the windows were busted, and the door hung perpetually open, connected to its frame by only one hinge. As the King looked on an unhygienic old beggar stopped in front of it, considered entering, and thought better of it.

It would do.

Inside, the King spent his remaining cash on booze and a room. The dour innkeeper wordlessly handed him a key, which slid from the King's grasp when he first tried to take it. It was filthy.

Sitting in his cramped room, getting dripped on by the leaky ceiling, he had begun drinking the tenth of seventeen flagons when he heard the distinct sound of foreplay coming from the adjoining room. He scowled. How fitting, that the last thing he heard was a reminder of what so doggedly eluded him.

He started knocking back number eleven, and paused. Perhaps it was the alcohol, but one of the voices began to sound decidedly familiar. He listened closer, and nearly tumbled from his stool in disbelief. It was impossible. After all he had endured, to think that here, in this grimy inn…no. His dismal frame of mind was playing tricks on him, nothing more.

The voice spoke again, and now he was dead certain. Immediately he made his decision. The King stumbled into the hall and kicked his neighbour's door in.

"Is someone there?" a wavering voice inquired from within.

The King peered in to behold three elderly women playing Bridge. "Sorry," he said. "Wrong room." He gently closed their door.

He staggered down the hall and kicked his other neighbour's door in.

Inside, he found Alice with another man. They were drinking port. The King roared.

"*What is the meaning of this?*"

Alice cleared her throat loudly. "Well, allow me to clarify. I met this man last week, and now we're going to make love.

"You're interrupting," she added.

Alice's new lover was squinting hard at the King. "Hey, isn't that the same guy who likes to walk around in drag?"

The King's drunken mind raced, even now unwilling to accept the obvious conclusion.

"Alice," he said, "what went wrong? Was it that horrid story in the Crier? It's completely untrue!"

"No, that wasn't it," Alice said. "The story was pretty amusing, though."

"But did you see my ad?"

"I saw it."

"And?"

"And it's the same thing I've heard from a million other guys, okay? I find you boring, Your Majesty. Dull. Shallow. What's the word I'm looking for here? One-dimensional. And you're a terrible kisser. Face it—you were yesterday's fling. Jason is the man of today." She smiled at the other man.

For a few seconds, Jason returned the smile. Then he frowned. "I'm the man of tomorrow too, right? And the next day?"

"Um…" Alice mumbled, but was spared having to respond by the King, who threw himself out of the window. This was of little consequence, as the inn only had one floor.

"Right, now where were we?" Alice said.

This scene will end now.

an indefinite period of time later. What is time, anyway? Suffice it to say the King spent it terribly depressed, and for the most part, drunk. If you really need some sort of reference, then it might be useful to know the opening scene, the one with the glassblower, had occurred by now. Satisfied?

The famous doctor, alchemist and knight stood at his window and studied the approaching figure with increasing confusion. Unless his three professions had at last relieved him of his mental faculties, Sir Forsythe was certain the visitor could only be the King. Except, Forsythe could conjecture no plausible reason for a visit. The King was never ill (much to the Kingdom's misfortune), possessed all his hair, and rarely needed saving from dragons.

"Welcome, Your Majesty," Forsythe said when the monarch entered his cottage.

The King stumbled close enough that Forsythe could feel his respiration.

"Is that cabernet sauvignon on your breath?" he asked politely.

"It was red."

"Yes. Can I help you with anything?"

"I hope so. I'm feeling a little under the weather."

"That's strange for you, Your Majesty. What are the symptoms?"

The King walked to an end table and dropped a piece of paper on it. "This poem," he said, and put a hand over his heart. "A sharp pain in my chest," he continued, holding up a flask. "And a strong inclination to drink. A lot."

Forsythe joined the monarch at the table, picking up the poem. It was a haiku:

Beer: my only friend.
Wine's good, too. So is liquor.
You are a harlot.

"Hmm." Sir Forsythe deliberated for a moment. "It appears you are in love, sire."

"I know. Can you fix it?"

"It isn't a disease."

The King regarded him incredulously. "You're a hack."

"Maybe. But I sincerely doubt it."

"Can't you at least tell me why it's happening?"

"As a matter of fact, I can. I dabble in biology, you see. I would have been an anatomist, but I rather have too many professions as it is."

The King waited.

"Humans feel love due to an evolutionary drive to reproduce. Biologically speaking it's extremely complicated, but essentially, there are a whole mess of hormones released, which trigger a whole mess of other hormones, until suddenly you're head over heels. Which is where your head is normally situated, mind you, but you get my meaning."

"Can't the hormones be removed?"

Forsythe considered this. "It would require an operation that would almost certainly prove fatal." He paused. "No, that's wrong. It would definitely kill you."

The King's face lit up, as though struck by an epiphany. He shook Sir Forsythe's hand vigorously. "Thank you. You've been a tremendous help."

With that, the ruler tottered out the door.

time passes

"Come to Devil's Drop at sunset," said the note waiting for Alice at the squalid inn she frequented, "or suffer the wrath of the monarchy."

That the monarchy had very little wrath left to dispense was a fact not lost on Alice. She was bored, however, having dumped Jason. She decided to comply.

Devil's Drop was a sheer cliff surrounded by desolation. Many an old story, told at fireside to credulous youngsters, used it as a setting for its climax. After today, Alice would wholly appreciate why.

It is hardly worth mentioning that as soon as Alice left the inn, it began to rain.

At the bottom of Devil's Drop, Alice found a wizened old man sitting in a rocking chair. He puffed industriously on a pipe.

"Don't go up," he counselled.

"Who are you?" Alice asked him. "What are you doing here?"

"Just my job, ma'am."

"And what would that be?"

He puffed on his pipe. "Telling folks not to go up."

She arched an eyebrow. "And you get paid for that?"

"A decent wage, yes." He blew a smoke ring. "Respectable hours, too. There are two other fellows, and we all take shifts. There's Benny—he smokes cigarettes—and Abram. He's a cigar man."

"Who would pay someone to do that?"

"Actually, it's funny you should ask, ma'am. He just went up to the Drop. I told him not to—not that it was really necessary—but he went up all the same."

Alice started up the steep incline. "Don't say I didn't warn you!" the old man called after her. "I'll lose my job if you do!"

It was hard going. The rain continued to pour, and the terrain was treacherous. Several times Alice nearly slipped on loose silt.

"This better be amusing," she growled under her breath.

If Alice's idea of 'amusing' included shameless melodrama and partial nudity, she was in for a real treat.

"I don't care if you're royalty," she said when she reached the summit and found the King lying at the edge of the Drop. "Put your shirt back on."

Oh well.

A man unknown to Alice stepped forward. He was missing an eye, and had a hump on his back. He lurched when he walked, for effect.

"But if he puts his shirt back on," the strange man rasped, "how will we proceed with the operation?"

Lighting rent the sky, and thunder crashed.

"Who asked you?" Alice retorted. She digested what he had said. "Operation? What operation? Who's operating on whom?"

"You are, Alice. On me." The King's tone was flat and dead. Even more disconcerting, he sounded sober. "You are going to remove my heart." He raised his hand dramatically, revealing a gleaming surgical scalpel.

A horrified silence reigned as Alice stared disbelievingly at the King.

"No," she said.

"I don't want it, you understand," the King continued as if she hadn't spoken. "It doesn't work anymore. It's broken. You might as well have it."

More silence. "You're nuts," Alice said finally.

"Do you wish to know *why* it's broken, Alice?"

"Not particularly."

"Do you wish to know *why* I'm lying here in the dirt with no shirt on?"

"No."

"You did this, Alice. I loved you, and you cast my love aside. So remove my heart—go ahead! Take it! Mount it on your wall as a trophy!"

Alice studied her nails.

"*Argh!*" the King screeched. "*You can't just brush off love! I'm a bloody King!*"

Abruptly, he moved the scalpel until it hovered above his heart. It gleamed ominously. The King whispered, "Very well. I'll just have to do it myself."

Alice blinked.

The King's hand trembled.

Alice yawned.

"Well?" the King said finally.

"Well, what?"

"Well, what do you have to say to that!"

"Not a lot."

"I'll do it!"

"Go ahead."

The King's hand trembled some more. The scalpel lowered. At last, he dropped it to his side with a sigh. He was a little embarrassed.

"All right. You win, okay? I wasn't going to do it."

THE END.

The King
of
Diamonds

The King's continued existence was an astonishing phenomenon.

Only nine months had passed since he lay—supine, vul-
nerable and half-naked—on a craggy precipice named Devil's Drop.
Also present were the love of his life, a man with one eye, and a
gleaming, diamond-edged scalpel.

He still hadn't quite come to terms with it all.

Last he'd heard of Alice, she'd become a prostitute. She now ran a
lucrative service two streets over from the Royal Square. Although
the King enjoyed the buffet of slurs now applicable to her, it did little
to ease his anguish, especially when he recalled a certain newspaper
article printed shortly after he met Alice. Nine months later, he had
yet to live it down.

The one-eyed man with the hump had become an expert dart
thrower, winning tournament after tournament in taverns and bars all
across the Kingdom. "Depth perception only gets in the way," he
was widely credited with saying. Aspiring dart throwers from all over
went on extensive pilgrimages to absorb his teachings.

The scalpel had gone on to be owned by the celebrated Sir
Forsythe, who, despite already being a doctor, alchemist and knight,
decided to become an anatomist after all. He used it during countless
life-saving operations.

The King just drank a lot.

One learned much in nine months. For instance, he discovered
that while mead was good for nursing a mild depression, if he really
wanted to get suicidal hard liquor was the answer. He also learned

that whether he made an effort as King had very little effect on whether his Kingdom prospered. Actually, it seemed to fare better without his intervention.

The only lesson that meant anything to the King, however, was one concerned with *l'amour*. That is, he realized he'd been going about it all wrong. Women weren't interested in a man who listened to them, or cared how they felt. Sensitivity, good looks, charm— evidently, these things counted for little. Women responded to one thing only: extravagant displays of wealth.

It was with this resolution that he entered a long room reeking of alcohol and sweat. The King was searching for commitment. The King was searching for a soul mate.

The King was barhopping.

*

As he approached, he watched her nervously. He had never done this before. She was pretty. She had shiny black hair, and around her neck drooped a dead animal. A mink, unless the King missed his guess. He hoped its death had been painless.

He forced himself to imagine spending his life with this woman. He tried to picture her caring for his child. The mink stared at him lifelessly.

"Greetings," said the King. "What are you called?"

"Greta. You?"

"I'm the King."

Greta didn't seem impressed.

"Aren't you going to buy me a drink?" she said.

The King raised his eyebrows. "A drink? A mere drink? Such a piddling expenditure would be insulting to a woman of your beauty and social graces. Milady, I intend to buy you the entire bar. Bartender!"

The bartender, also the proprietor, waddled over. He wasn't a very big man by any means, though he waddled all the same.

"What can I do for you?"

"Good sir, I would like to purchase this establishment. Name your price."

"Not for sale."

The King fell silent, nonplussed.

He began again, slower: "How about seventeen acres of land, and three score slaves with which to cultivate it?"

"I said it's not for sale."

The King could see the man required a little encouragement. He leaned closer. "I can have you executed, you know. I can, and I will."

"That's well and good," the bartender answered, "but you'd also have to execute my wife. She gets the bar after I die. It's in my will."

"That," the King said, "can be arranged."

"And I suppose my best friend would want it after that. He lives two doors down. You'd have to execute him, too."

"Is that all?"

"No. My friend has a brother—Ralph the Nomad. He wanders around some three-hundred leagues north of here. You'd need to track him down and execute him after you behead my friend."

"Hmm. Indeed?"

"Yep. And Ralph has a distant cousin with a knack for mixing Bloody Marys, who's always wanted to—"

"That's quite all right, sir," the King said, failing to make eye contact. "I just recollected my executioner is on sick leave, and therefore unable to operate a guillotine. Quite a pity. I suppose you may keep your bar."

The bartender waddled off.

"Well!" said the King under Greta's derisive gawk. "This is awkward."

For a time, they said nothing.

"So, uh, what do you do for a living?" Greta finally asked.

"Me? Oh. I'm a monarch."

"Ah," Greta said. "How's that going for you?"

"Not bad. I tell people what to do, and if they refuse, I have them hanged. When my executioner isn't laid up, that is."

"I see."

"What about you?"

"I go from bar to bar and try to attract men with lots of money. When I meet one who's rich and willing, I marry him. Then I spend his money."

"Isn't that like prostitution?"

"It's exactly like prostitution. But because there's a ceremony involved, they call it matrimony. And this way I don't have to wear sleazy outfits."

The King eyed her attire dubiously.

"Greta," he began sadly, "I don't think it's going to work out between us."

Greta would get over it.

*

When the fiddler-for-hire arrived at the throne room, he found the King depressingly sober.

Bottles of expensive wine were strewn around the chamber, unopened. A corkscrew lay within inches of the King's left foot. He had *tried* to get disgracefully inebriated—he really had—yet so great was his despondency he lacked the motivation to consume a single drop.

The fiddler stood uncertainly in the entranceway.

"I've never been to a wedding, you know." The King's declaration echoed hollowly off the marble.

The fiddler regarded him blankly. "Oh?"

"If you've never actually witnessed something, you don't have to believe in it. Isn't that right? Outside of religion, of course."

"I suppose that's one way of—"

"Because I am having extreme difficulty understanding how the permanent union of a man and a woman could ever work. And since I've never been to a wedding, it's much simpler for me to think them imaginary."

Changing the subject, the fiddler handed the monarch an issue of the Kingdom Crier. "I'm here to apply for the fiddler position. I'm Frederick."

The King studied the newspaper. "But this ad ran two years ago. No one was interested."

"Two years, yes. That's how long it took to learn the fiddle."

Frederick had finally won the King's full attention.

"You—you mean to say—"

"I saw the ad and decided to learn the fiddle. I needed the cash."

"What have you been doing for money till now?"

"Playing the oboe."

Though he didn't know it, Frederick already had the job. And when he took his fiddle from its case and produced the sweetest melody the King had ever heard—well, that helped, too.

*

Frederick's music was mesmerizing. The King knew this because nobody at the ball he had thrown to celebrate his new fiddler was talking with one another—or with the King. Instead they gazed at Frederick and his fiddle; listened intently to the divine melodies there produced.

The fiddler left off for a coffee break, and conversation gradually resumed. The King wandered among his guests, fulfilling his duties as gracious host.

"Don't scuff your feet!" he snapped at a passing nobleman. "You'll mark the hardwood!"

The King rarely used the ballroom, and so it was slightly less dilapidated than the rest of his castle. It was still rather dilapidated. The paint was peeling from the walls, and the ancient chandelier looked in danger of falling. He grimaced at the cacophony of squeaks the floor produced as his guests milled about.

In the crowd's shuffle Sir Forsythe appeared before him, toting a glass of brandy.

"Good evening, Your Majesty. Your new musician plays like a virtuoso. Where did you find him?"

"In the exotic jungles of the south, while hunting a lion that was troubling some villagers there." The King had never been to a jungle, but the accomplished Sir Forsythe made him feel inferior. He felt justified in obscuring the truth a little.

"Fascinating. By the way, Your Majesty, I must thank you for the scalpel you gave me. It's first-rate."

The King gestured airily. "A mere knickknack. In any case, I felt I should repay you for—well, in retrospect, you didn't do anything, did you? Can I have my scalpel back?"

"No," Sir Forsythe said, and dissolved back into the crowd.

The next face the King encountered was as hateful as it was familiar.

"Duke Edward," the King spat. "Funny. I don't recall inviting you."

The Editor of the Kingdom Crier smiled broadly at the King. "That's a relief, Your Majesty, because I don't recall *being* invited. I'm glad to find my memory is as functional as it always was."

"How did you get in? You aren't on the guest list."

"Yes, your doorman mentioned something along those lines, but he seemed too busy getting my autograph to turn me away. Besides, I have a press pass." He indicated his head, where a stylish fedora sat. The word 'press' was stencilled across a slip of paper stuck in its band.

"You won't find any news here," the King said. "Only the appreciation of good music. You know—culture. Are you familiar with the term?"

"Your idiocy alone makes for an excellent story, Your Highness. At any rate, you're bound to slip up. You can barely manage your sock drawer, let alone a roomful of drunken nobles. As for your fiddler, you have me to thank that you ever laid eyes on him. It was my newspaper he read your ad in, after all."

"That ad cost me thirty thousand pounds!"

"Business is business, sire."

The King drew himself up. "The only thing I have to thank you for is a reputation as a cross dresser. And by thank, I mean murder."

"Ah, yes," the Editor said. "I think now would be the appropriate time to introduce you to the soldier I was talking with before you...introduced yourself into the conversation." He beckoned to a young man wearing a black uniform who waited politely nearby. "Private Reginald, this is the ruler of this Kingdom. He likes to wear women's clothing."

Private Reginald tried to maintain a courteous level of interest. "Is that right? I have a friend who's into the same sort of thing."

"Really?" said the King.

"Yes, quite." The soldier faltered. "Er...she's a girl."

The King turned red. Refusing to let Edward ruin things, he pressed on. "Who do you work for?" he asked the soldier. "This Kingdom has no standing army."

"Oh, I'm not from this Kingdom. Actually, the forces I'm with are about to begin a new campaign. Our commander let us take the last

56

night off before the attack, so I decided to come and see whether this Kingdom knows how to make merry."

"And do we?"

"Without a doubt, sire. Plenty of good booze. I'm rather impressed."

The King's pride swelled, along with his opinion of the young soldier. "How go preparations for the campaign, then, Private?"

"Amazingly well, Your Highness. It's almost too easy. We're camped right over the hill from our enemy, and he doesn't even realize it. From what I've heard, he's a real loon—completely ignorant about what's going on outside his own castle."

The King dipped his chin knowingly. "I've heard of such bungling rulers. I expect you'll find matters much more orderly here."

"I think I already have a good idea of that, Your Majesty."

The King beamed. "Enjoy yourself, Private." He re-entered the crowd, snubbing the Duke. His spirits were much higher.

After the King left, Duke Edward released a fit of pent-up mirth. "I told you it would be amusing. Quite a moron, isn't he?"

Private Reginald shook his head wonderingly. "How could a man like that possibly be allowed to run a Kingdom?"

"Well, that's just it—he *doesn't* run it. All he does is eat, sleep and have people executed. But nobody cares. I mean, sure—the public loves a scandal, and that's why the Crier does so well. They love hearing insignificant yet embarrassing details about his personal life, but his actual policies hold no interest for them. I once asked a peasant if he ever felt afraid of being executed, and he said no, because he never did anything wrong. He said his neighbour had been hanged, but he knew why—he said she'd been extremely annoying."

They sipped their cocktails and mulled this over.

"When does your General plan to commence the assault?" Duke Edward asked at length.

"Tomorrow, directly after noon."

"Splendid. Listen, can you deliver this note to him?"

At that moment Frederick resumed playing, and once again all conversation evaporated.

This was fine by the King—he didn't much like conversation. Or people, for that matter. Except perhaps the attractive woman staring at him from across the ballroom—the only guest not paying attention to Frederick. The King decided he would probably like her very much.

"What's your name?" the King asked her once he had walked to the bar, knocked back some ale, administered breath freshener and returned to the crowd.

"Alice."

The King retreated three steps. "Indeed?"

"Um, yes. Is that okay?"

"I'm not sure."

This was already very awkward.

"What's wrong with my name?" said Alice, slightly put off.

"There's nothing *wrong* with it, per se. It's just that speaking it causes me excruciating pain. You see, there's this other maiden I know, who also—well, it's a long story." The King smiled sheepishly.

Alice harrumphed.

"Listen," the King said, becoming desperate. "For the purposes of this conversation, can I call you something else?"

"You want me to change my name?"

"Only briefly."

"And what would you have me change it to? Do I get to choose?"

"Of course!" The King grinned widely.

"How about Kandice?"

"Hmm," said the King. "No. It's too similar."

"You are unbearable. Fran?"

"Too ordinary."

"Eliza!" she shouted, at the end of her patience.

"Yes! That's it! For the duration of our discourse, you shall be known as Eliza."

"In that case, you can call me Alice. I'm leaving." And she did.

The King would have been distraught, but he was too busy admiring Eliza's retreating posterior.

His guests departed within the hour, and the King retired to his bedchamber, grinning foolishly at nothing. Predictably, he had fallen for Eliza quite thoroughly.

*

58

Rain beat against the windows, as usual, but for once the King didn't mind.

"I met the most exquisite female last night," he informed Frederick loudly.

The fiddler halted his morning practice with a grimace.

"Indeed?" he said, feigning interest.

"Indeed!" the King said, and went on to describe his encounter in painful detail.

"What was her name?" Frederick asked when he finished.

"Eliza," said the King after very little consideration.

"Hmm. Strange. The woman you describe sounds vaguely familiar."

Perhaps the irony in Frederick's statement will become evident a little later.

*

The King was talking to his mirror. Since his advisor died he hadn't anyone to counsel him, and so he often solicited advice from his reflection. It rarely gave any.

"Now what?" he asked it.

He dimly recalled finding the last girl he'd blindly pursued in a second-rate inn with another man. However, though they had only exchanged one hundred and twenty-seven words, he could tell Eliza was nothing like Alice. She would never pretend interest in him while fraternizing with another man. She was a virtuous, ball-faring lady.

"I'm looking for the bathroom," said Eliza's reflection, standing in the doorway.

Shooting himself a last appraising glance, the King turned about and cocked a suggestive eyebrow.

"Are you sure that's all you're looking for?"

"I could also use a job and new shoes," said Eliza. "But of these three, the bathroom is the most urgent."

Frowning, he directed her accordingly. Despite the pride he took in the castle's facilities, the King thought this an odd path to his heart.

It occurred to him to wonder briefly why she was here.

He took a seat and awaited her return—in vain. After some time Frederick's music reached him from down the hall, and he followed the melody to the fiddler's room.

"Frederick, have you seen a tall brunette around? Sort of elegant, with—"

Utter shock cut short his words. Frederick *had* seen a tall, elegant brunette. She was currently nestled in his lap in a way that was anything but platonic. Some distracted fraction of the King's thoughts marvelled at Frederick's continued ability to play the fiddle. A much larger portion was devoted to nooses and guillotines and the like.

"Hello, Your Majesty," Frederick said, adding speech to his performance. "Meet Alice. Alice, meet the ruler of—"

"We've met," said Eliza.

"Oh," said Frederick, and carried on with fiddling (both musical and otherwise).

The King looked on uncertainly. "Who's Alice?" he said.

*

He bade the entwined pair a hasty farewell and fled through the castle corridors. No one asked him what the matter was, because no one was there to ask. As a reward for throwing such a smashing ball the previous night, he had given his staff a holiday. (It was the first they'd ever enjoyed in his employ.) Aside from the three of them, the castle was empty.

It wasn't fair. He couldn't stomach it. It was just like his luck, to arrange for his new employee and his new lover to be sweethearts.

His aimless fleeing brought him to his bedchambers. He flung open the window and, upon the sill, buried his head in his arms. For once it wasn't raining, and a warm summer breeze tugged at his sleeve, as if to ask him what all the fuss was about.

The King supposed, in one sense, he should be grateful. The agonizing ordeal with Alice had lasted days and days, but it seemed his Eliza troubles had begun and concluded in a tidy seventeen hours. Besides, his heart had already been obliterated once. What were a few more sledgehammer blows?

A trumpet sounded in the distance. The King looked up, unenthused. His interest grew when he discerned a flood of movement on the apex of Shepherd's Hill. He squinted. A swarm of black-clad figures was cresting the summit, only to rush down the side nearest the King. It seemed to be some sort of a parade, or a marathon, or perhaps a...

(The King's mouth fell open.)

...a vast host of armed warriors, dressed in the same uniform Private Reginald had worn.

The trumpet blared again, inspiring the King once more to scamper down the hallways. This time, he screamed uncontrollably.

"Your Majesty!" Frederick called as the King ran past the room in which he and Eliza cuddled. "Whatever is the matter?"

The King entered the room and paused to catch his breath, holding up a finger. Finally, he was ready.

"What is it?" Frederick said urgently.

The King's brow furrowed. "I can't remember."

"Oh."

"It can't have been very important. I'll let you know if I recall." The King left the room again.

Frederick and Eliza returned to snuggling.

The King came barrelling back in. "I remember now!" he shrieked. "*Invaders! Approaching the castle!*"

Frederick jumped up. "Is the drawbridge closed?"

The King thought this over.

"No!"

"Then let's go!" They dashed out of the room.

"Bring your fiddle!" said the King. They dashed back. Frederick tore open the case and extracted his instrument.

They dashed out again.

Downstairs, the attackers were already rushing into the entrance foyer.

"Hey!" Frederick shouted from the stairs, his voice cracking. The King cowered behind him. "Get out of here!" Frederick brandished the fiddle.

"Assail them!" ordered the King from over the fiddler's shoulder.

By now completely pale, Frederick proceeded hesitantly down the staircase. "Hey!" he shouted again. He swung the instrument in a clumsy arc.

The black-uniformed soldiers drew up hastily. "Hold it, boys! He's got a fiddle."

"That's right!" Frederick said.

"Is that a Stradivarius?" asked another soldier, who wielded a broadsword.

"Er, no," the fiddler said. "It's a replica."

"Skilfully crafted, though," said the swordsman. The invaders all agreed.

Another piped up. "Hey, now, you're not going to hit us with that, are you?"

Frederick faltered.

"I've been thinking about it!"

"But you might damage it," a thoughtful young corporal observed.

"That's possible, yes."

"You shouldn't jeopardize a decent piece of equipment like that."

"I've taken leave of my senses!" Frederick said, gaining momentum.

"Instruments like that are hard to come by nowadays."

"I'll just have to do without!" the fiddler said, a wild gleam in his eyes.

The soldiers muttered among themselves. "Bloody maniacal," one said. "Not a shred of respect for good craftsmanship," said another.

The corporal cleared his throat. "If you're not going to be reasonable, then we'll have to. Come on, men. We'll find another way in. On the double, now."

The soldiers filed out in an orderly fashion. The King rushed up to the winch that controlled the drawbridge and cranked it for all his worth.

King and fiddler leaned panting against the blessedly vertical wooden plane.

"Play me a mournful tune," the King said.

*

62

The occupying army seemed content to wait outside the castle indefinitely. They brought playing cards, and the sound of their raucous gambling often drifted through the windows.

Remaining inside the castle were the King, Frederick, Eliza, and a dwindling supply of alcohol.

Food stocks were low, too.

The King sighed. Why had he ever become King, anyhow? People were forever trying to blame, maim or trap him inside a castle without any food. The hours were lousy, too.

Becoming King had seemed like a good idea when he was attending university. He had devoured histories of past monarchies voraciously. He fancied himself similar to all the good kings, and different from all the bad. For instance, he was nothing like Samuel the Slaughterer. He shared his taste for executions, certainly, but every man has his vices.

"I need an army," the King said as he gazed out the seventh-floor window at a smoking cottage. Whenever the invaders required supplies, they simply razed another peasant's hovel after taking all it contained. "Would you sign up?" he asked Frederick.

The fiddler took a long draught before answering. They were drinking the last of the brandy and contemplating their situation, since there was nothing else they could do about it.

"I'm a musician, Your Majesty. Not a fighter."

"You did splendidly in the foyer the other day."

The fiddler shook his head. "Only because I defended against idiots."

"Idiots, or extremely idealistic music connoisseurs."

"Maybe you shouldn't have sent all the guards away."

They mulled this over. The King finished his drink.

"I wish there were more peasants," he said at length.

"Why? Do you think you could recruit them?"

"No. But they make such excellent fodder."

Frederick peered over the rooftops. "The Kingdom Crier still hasn't been touched. You'd think a place like that would be the first to go. Aren't the third and fourth floors purely residential? Imagine the food."

The King nodded. He thought back to the ball, when he'd found Duke Edward speaking with Private Reginald. "I'd like to know what the headlines are saying."

The King was mistaken. He wouldn't like that at all.

*

Nature let forth a stentorian roar, and the King could only obey.

The castle's facilities consisted of three restrooms—marked *Lords, Ladies,* and *Kings.* He entered the appropriate door, took care of business, and stepped out again. Eliza was waiting outside.

"Er, hello."

"What's it like in there?" she asked, looking past him.

"Lonely. Would you like to see?"

They went in, holding their noses.

"What's that?" Eliza asked nasally. She indicated a strange porcelain bowl that looked like a toilet, but wasn't one.

"It's called a bidet."

"What does it do?"

The King whispered in her ear. Startled, she drew back and regarded him incredulously. "Are you serious? Do you...do you ever use it?"

"I did. Once. The novelty wears off rather quickly."

"I see."

Other than the bidet, the King's lavatory contained sumptuous couches, a fountain-sized bath, a sizable throne (er, toilet) and scented towels. "It's really just another washroom," he said modestly.

"And you're really just another monarch."

The King opened his mouth to protest.

"Your Majesty," Eliza interrupted.

"Yes?"

"I've been wondering about something. At the ball you held for Frederick...did you feel something?"

The King frowned. "A little tipsy, I suppose."

Eliza shook her head. "No, I meant something between us."

He studied her, mystified. "Like what?"

"A little like this," she said, leaning in and kissing him softly. "But not nearly so strong."

64

At length, the King found his voice. "Now you mention it," he said, gazing nervously into her sky-coloured eyes, "yes, I did. Almost immediately."

"Okay. Just checking." Eliza exited the bathroom.

The King sat heavily on a nearby silk couch. He considered the fact that he, Frederick, and Frederick's girlfriend were all trapped inside the same castle, and that Frederick's girlfriend had just come on to him.

This was about to get very awkward.

*

In the small hours of the morning the King slouched low in his throne and wondered what to do. Nearly a month had passed since his castle was besieged, and still no reason was forthcoming.

Another matter that showed no sign of resolving itself concerned he and Eliza. They continued to conduct their unplanned reunions, doing things a girlfriend should not do with anyone other than her significant other. Frederick remained oblivious.

As well, lack of food was beginning to displace lack of alcohol as their primary dilemma. This was perhaps the most worrying.

Without warning, a darkly dressed man dropped from an upper window and skulked across the throne room. He peered into the hallway, his back turned to the throne.

"Excuse me?" said the King.

The man whirled around, a blade flashing in his hand. Spotting the King on his throne, he gave a relieved sigh, and tucked the weapon away. "You startled me."

"Apologies," the King said, bewildered.

"That's fine. Could you tell me the quickest route to your storeroom?"

"Down the hall, second passageway on your left. Take the stairs at the end."

"Thanks." The man turned to leave.

"Do you mind my asking who you are?"

The man turned back. "Not at all. Name's Sam. I'm a spy. You'll be the Majesty, then?"

"Uh, yes. How did you get in?"

Sam smiled. "There's a handy drain pipe that runs right up to that busted window, there." He pointed. "Your stable master told us about it. He says you've neglected to have it repaired for going on a year, now."

"My stable master?"

"The one and only. He was caught outside when we arrived, and we gave him a choice: defect or die. It wasn't a hard decision. He said you don't pay him near enough to expire in your service."

"Is this your first time in here?"

"Oh, yes, of course. It's my first time."

The King stopped holding his breath.

"My mates have been in and out plenty, though."

The King wheezed.

"We've kept pretty up-to-date on your stores. You're running a little low now, aren't you?"

"You could say that, yes." The King paused. "I'm famished, actually."

"Pity. Well then, I'll just be popping off to your stores. Not that I don't believe you, mind. I still have to check. Blasted bureaucracy, right?"

"Right," the King said. He frowned. "But if you have such unlimited access, then why don't you simply let the rest of the army in?"

The spy appraised him wonderingly. "That's an excellent idea!" The King winced. "I'll have to run it by the General."

"Um, listen, I think it might be prudent to apprehend you now."

"It might be prudent, yes. If you could manage it. I have my doubts, though. I do have a rapier."

"I'm going to try anyway," said the King. He started for the intruder.

In seconds, he lay on the floor with a blade to his neck. "I'm sorry about this, sire. Royalty shouldn't try military's patience, that's all." Using curtains, the spy securely trussed and gagged him. He flashed another smile. "Hang tight, Your Highness. I'll release you when I leave."

*

The following morning the King accosted Frederick in a corridor. His hands and ankles still ached from being so tightly bound.

"Lock all the entrances to the castle from the inside as well as out. Then give me the key."

The fiddler scratched his head. "Are you trying to prevent us from leaving? It's not as if we're particularly eager to. There's a forest of steel out there."

"Don't question. Just do it."

That night, the King waited under the broken window.

"*Ugh*," he said when the spy landed on him.

"This again, Your Majesty? It's getting rather tiresome." The spy pinned him down as he tore the curtains from yet another window.

He was about to put the gag in place when the King recovered his breath, and managed: "Can we talk about this?"

The spy hesitated. "I'm afraid not, sire. You can't be trusted, and therefore must be tied up. You tried to capture me, remember?" He moved the gag closer.

"No!" the King said. "No. Not that. I mean this whole business. The siege."

The spy fiddled with the rag in consternation. "We *could* talk," he said at length, "but I don't think it would amount to much. I'm just a spy."

"Then can you bear a message for your commander?"

The spy considered this a moment. "What is it?"

The King resisted a strong inclination to say something rude. "Just that I'd like to speak with him about all this. In person."

The spy consented to bear the King's message and finally tied the gag, again promising to free the King upon his departure. Twenty-four hours later saw them in exactly the same position.

"What did he say?" the King asked moments before his captor gagged him for the third time in three nights.

"He'd be delighted to."

*

Eliza lounged in the King's lap, who in turn lounged on the throne. She kissed him passionately.

There was a cough from the entranceway. They both turned their heads.

Frederick had entered the throne room.

"What are you two doing?"

The King and Eliza stammered in harmony.

"I—" Eliza began, her arms still entwined about the King's neck.

"She—" the King agreed, his hand tangled in Eliza's hair.

"There was something in his teeth," Eliza said. "I was helping him get it out."

The King stared at her incredulously.

"Using your tongue?" the fiddler asked.

"Um, yes."

Frederick's brow furrowed. "That works, then, does it?" He moved closer for inspection.

"Like a charm," Eliza answered. She nudged the King, and he smiled toothily.

The fiddler could see she spoke the truth—there was nothing lodged in the King's teeth.

"That's useful. You'll have to do the same for me, next time I eat corn on the cob. Always gets stuck between my bloody molars."

"Um, sure."

"Great. Anyhow. Carry on." Frederick left the throne room.

The King and Eliza shared a flabbergasted look.

A short while later, they resumed kissing.

*

The General was a portly old bureaucrat named Percy. He entered the castle through a little-used side door. He didn't shake the rain from his coat. This was because it wasn't raining, and hadn't been since the occupying army arrived. It only stood to reason the King-dom would finally enjoy good weather only when the King was trapped indoors.

Frederick stood by with a crossbow in case any soldiers attempted to enter, though he knew not what would happen if they did. He was about as acquainted with the use of a crossbow as a dormouse is with the use of Beethoven.

Eliza also stood nearby, studying her nails.

General Percy didn't appear to mind being unaccompanied. In fact, he didn't appear to mind much of anything. He smiled perpetually, and was in possession of a throaty, grating laugh, which he made liberal use of. Despite his host's palpable hostility, he insisted on shaking hands. The King immediately wiped himself off on his clothes, grimacing.

All four retired to the dining chamber to confer.

"Parley!" General Percy cried, as if naming the world's finest luxury. "Can't get enough of parley. It's my favourite part of conflict."

An icy silence held sway.

General Percy spoke again, seemingly impervious to social awkwardness. "There's always such superb brandy at parleys. The enemy is forever trying to butter you up." He gazed up and down the empty dining table. "Excuse me, but where's the brandy?"

"Why are you here?" the King asked coldly.

"Why am I here?" he repeated. "Because you invited me, I suppose."

"Why is your *army* here," Eliza said.

"Why is my army *here,* young lady? My army isn't here! They're waiting outside the—"

"*Why is my castle under siege!*" roared the King.

The commander tittered, apparently interpreting the King's increase in volume as part of some larger joke. "Well that's simple!" he said jovially. The King sat up in his seat, eager to finally be given an explanation. "It's under siege because you'd leave if it wasn't."

The King lunged for General Percy's throat. Frederick intervened just in time, barely restraining the livid monarch.

The General finally seemed to notice something amiss. He drew himself up indignantly. "I feel like you're making me out to be the enemy."

"You *are* the enemy!" all three shouted in unison. Frederick barely restrained the King as he threw himself forward once more.

General Percy nodded slowly. "True enough, true enough." He scratched his chin. "I'll tell you why I brought my army to this particular Kingdom then, shall I?"

Silence gave consent.

"Well, we were all set to do battle with another Kingdom, a nice ways off to the east. Both sides were raring to go. We'd sharpened our respective swords, filled our respective quivers, and honed our respective resolves, But suddenly that Kingdom's government decided it didn't want to go to war, after all. Decided what we were fighting over wasn't really worth it!"

"What were you fighting over?" asked Eliza.

"Bugger if I can remember. Anyhow, there I was, sitting on five hundred battle-thirsty hooligans, and with no battle to lead them to. What was I supposed to tell them? That they should just—just go back to their families? Go back to being peaceful, after all that sword sharpening? Preposterous!"

"So what did you tell them?"

"Nothing, at first. In fact, it's what someone told *me* that made the difference. A man from sort of traveling guild said that far off to the west lay a Kingdom so backward the media controlled the King, instead of vice versa. Devoid of military, he said, and ripe for the taking. One thing led to another, and here I am. Waiting for the papaya to fall from the proverbial tree."

Frederick found the need to restrain his employer had arisen again.

"Leave my castle," the King hissed. "Leave or I'll disembowel you."

They all went down to the side door, Frederick keeping a close eye on his liege. As they traversed the corridors, the General offered advice on how to improve the castle's "ghastly" interior design. The King thought about how nice the General's head would look on a spike.

General Percy turned to the King just before leaving. "Oh, Your Majesty. I almost forgot. I was speaking with a friend of yours just before coming. Duke Edward says hello."

With that, he left.

*

The King sat with his hands folded and stared dejectedly at the empty dining table. The trio trapped inside the castle were dispirited usually, infiltrated frequently and surrounded constantly. Above all, they were hungry.

Matters had worsened until a single, inescapable truth was realized: they had to eat. To the King's mind, there were three possible courses of action. He and Frederick could team up and eat Eliza, on the grounds that she was a girl. He and Eliza could get together and eat Frederick, on the grounds that he was a musician. Or Eliza and Frederick could join forces and eat the King, on the grounds that they were lovers—however unfaithful.

Eliza entered the dining chamber, setting a loaf of bread and a bottle of mead in front of him. "Dig in," she invited.

The King was dumbstruck. He stared hard at the food, afraid it might disappear if he looked away. A single syllable tumbled from his gaping mouth: "How?"

"Simple. I went to the market."

The King stood up and walked to a window. He looked down. The army still abided outside. He returned to the table.

He shrugged and began to eat.

"The soldiers aren't allowed to leave their camp, except to ransack houses," Eliza said. "As well, there are no women among them."

The King's confusion persisted. His hunger gradually abated, though, and only that truly concerned him.

Eliza continued to try and explain. "In exchange for even a glimpse of a female, they're willing to let one pass freely. So long as their commander isn't nearby, that is. He's a bit of a wet blanket."

"So you can go and come as you please?" the King asked around a mouthful of crumbs.

"More or less."

"But I have the keys to every exit."

"No you don't." She held up a jingling metal key ring. "I do."

He checked his belt. "So you do," he said. "When did you discover you could do this?"

"A couple days after they got here."

The King nearly choked. "*What?*"

She looked at him quizzically.

"You've been passing through their camp since they *arrived?*"

She nodded.

"What have you been doing out there?"

Her expression clouded. "I don't really want to talk about it."

"Does it involve food?"

"Well, I usually get something to eat, yes."

"But you don't bring any back?"

"No—I kept meaning to get around to it, but there are so many great deals in the marketplace right now, and they're kind of distracting. Turns out the soldiers are doing a lot for the economy, despite the razing. Look, I got this anklet."

The King looked down at his withering frame. He looked back at her. He heaved a resigned sigh, and continued eating.

"All right, fine," she said in a sudden explosion of breath. "I'll tell you what else I've been doing outside the castle."

The King looked at her blankly. He shrugged. "Okay."

*

The King stood at the foot of his bed, staring into a wooden chest. Inside lay the dress he yearned to have incinerated, but which he'd kept as a reminder of Duke Edward's treachery. Now he knew it to be his only method of accessing the rest of his Kingdom.

Scowling, he picked it up as one would a cobra.

He put it on.

The things he did for love.

*

The sun crawled across the sky, and, in passing, beat fiercely upon the King's uncovered head as he toiled up Mount High.

Perhaps certain bits of the previous sentence bear clarifying.

Mount High is named after its most striking feature. That it was being toiled up by the King can be explained by a local legend, which said that on the mountain's peak dwelled the Wisest Man Alive, who would exchange invaluable wisdom for the answer to one of his riddles.

All this mysticism was lost on the King. He did not climb Mount High in search of knowledge. He climbed it because Eliza had climbed it, and had been doing so regularly for the past month. As a sideline to invaluable wisdom, the Wisest Man Alive also offered counselling for a reasonable hourly fee.

The King looked up. Clouds obscured the peak. He looked at the ground. Clouds obscured that, too. This was irksome. He had never been faced with a problem he couldn't have executed.

Unless you counted Frederick, that is. Frederick, who had no idea what was happening between the King and Eliza. Frederick, the one person whose removal would solve everything. Frederick, the gods-forsaken Fiddler.

The King had learned much from his discussion with Eliza in the dining chamber. As it turned out, Eliza loved the King. It seemed her fiddling boyfriend meant little to her, in actuality. She would have left him long before, if not for one incidental detail.

"We tried breaking up once," Eliza said, "but as soon as we did, he was utterly unable to play his fiddle. It killed me, to see him pluck it discordantly like he'd never seen one before. We were back together in a week."

"That is the most ridiculous thing I've ever heard."

With this latest profession of love, Eliza pushed the King too far. His mind was made up. He'd resolved to destroy Eliza's relationship with Frederick by any means necessary. He'd resolved to end this once and for all.

He was going to bribe Eliza's therapist.

And that brings us to the peak of Mount High.

Panting, the King heaved himself onto the mountaintop. The mountain ended in a wide plateau, in the middle of which sat a modest cottage. Near its door the King spotted an axe and chopping block, though as far as he could see, no trees grew on the mountaintop. He wiped his sweaty brow. That the Wisest Man Alive might make frequent treks down the mountain was a notion the King's waning machismo forbade him to entertain.

Without further ado, the King strode up and pounded on the door.

"I can tell from the timbre of your knock you come seeking wisdom," said a voice that dripped with shrewdness. "But before entering, you must answer the following riddle."

The King eyed the nearby axe. He wandered in its general direction.

"What," the voice said, "has four wheels and flies?

The answering *thud*, though not the correct response, was taken just as seriously. The King brought the axe back for a second chop, but stopped when the door swung open.

The Wisest Man Alive looked just as you'd expect—old, bearded, and unhygienic. The corners of his eyes seemed perpetually crinkled in a smile, though their owner certainly wasn't smiling. "You could have had time to think about it," he said.

The King pushed past. He found the interior to be just as stereotypical as the old man. "Listen, I'm sorry about your door."

"No bother. Doors are a dime a dozen."

The King frowned. "I thought you might be angrier."

"It is unwise to be overly brash," the old man said, "with the man holding the axe."

He offered the King tea, which they drank at a rickety table covered in papers. The old man appeared to be working on something. "I have a lot of free time," he explained. For a while they eyed each other over the tops of their mugs. The King had yet to surrender the axe.

"What's your deal, anyhow?" he asked his host at last.

"Why, I'm the Wisest Man Alive."

"Yes, I know, but—it's a little bizarre, isn't it? I mean, how does one go about becoming the Wisest Man Alive? Are you self-proclaimed, or..." He trailed off doubtfully.

"Well, I used to be a philosopher. Quite renowned, actually."

"Oh?"

"Yes, quite so. But I went too far. Are you familiar with Descartes?"

"No."

"Really? How odd. Anyway, I endorsed views addressed in his work, you see. Except while he used them to gauge reality, I lived by them."

"I don't follow."

"Let's see if I can make it clearer: I didn't believe in a physical world."

"Ah."

"So when publishers came around to discuss buying my work, I treated them like figments of my imagination. They didn't like that. They stopped coming."

The King was unsure whether he should be offended. "And I'm a figment too, then?"

"Oh, no, certainly not," the Wisest Man Alive said. "A year of near starvation effectively realigned my views. I relocated to the top of Mount High to try and break into the counselling business. The title sort of happened naturally."

The King had begun to pace the room, idly swinging the axe by its haft. "Actually, that's why I'm here. Your counselling services." He paused. "This will take some time to explain."

"No need, Your Majesty. You're here about Alice—or Eliza, as you like to call her."

The King made a startled noise. "How do you even know who I am?"

"Being King involves a certain degree of publicity, sire. I recognized your face from the Kingdom Crier." He handed the King a recent copy.

"LICENTIOUS MONARCH STALKS INNOCENT MAIDEN," read the headline. Underneath was a painting of the King leering lecherously at Eliza from across the throne room.

"Good gods!" the King yelled. "How do they know that?"

"That you've been stalking young maidens?" the Wisest Man Alive asked with a twinkle in his eye.

The King reflected momentarily. "Actually, it's rather the other way around."

The old man chuckled. "The reason Duke Edward has such an intimate knowledge of the situation inside your castle is because he has an arrangement with General Percy. In return for keeping public opinion of you low, the commander has agreed to provide the Duke with intelligence garnered by his spies. He also promised not to torch the Kingdom Crier."

"What a pity," the King said. "Look, this is outrageous."

"And amusing. They've been running similar articles for weeks. Would you like to see some more headlines?"

"No." The King decided to get directly to the point. "I'm offering you dukedom over Mount High and the surrounding terrain, if you'll tell Eliza she should marry me."

Again the Wisest Man Alive chortled. "I don't think you understand how counselling works, Your Highness. I don't *tell* my patients to do anything. I simply make suggestions, and let them work things out for themselves."

The King gaped. "How much do you charge for this sham?"

"A reasonable fee."

"Ludicrous," the King declared. "Completely ludicrous. You must be hindering more than helping."

"As a matter of fact, the lady finds my services quite useful. Did you know she's developing an identity crisis? She can't decide if she's Eliza, Alice or someone else entirely."

The King cleared his throat.

"But what strikes me as truly interesting, Your Majesty, is that as far as I can see, *you* are in need of my counselling services far more than she. Your life is in utter disarray."

The King studied him uncertainly. "What do you mean?"

"Well, allow me to demonstrate. About a year ago you donated your entire fortune to charity. A month back, however, you were prepared to purchase an entire drinking establishment. What occurred in the intervening months?"

"I can't remember. I was drunk for nearly all of them. Perhaps I had a lucky streak of gambling."

The Wisest Man Alive sighed. "Let me try something else. Where do you receive visitors to the castle?"

"In the throne room, mostly."

"And what is a throne room, exactly?"

"It—why, it's a room with a throne in it."

"Very well. What colour is it painted?"

The King opened his mouth, but failed utterly to produce any sound. Finally he managed, "I have no idea."

"There are several such blind spots and discontinuities in your life, clearly visible to anyone paying attention."

The King considered this for a moment. "How much did you say you charge?"

"Never mind that. The counselling you need at present is of a military persuasion. I am willing to give it freely."

"*You* know how to end the siege?"

The Wisest Man Alive shrugged. "Like I said: when you live on top of a mountain, you have a lot of time to think."

"Go on."

The Wisest Man Alive chose this time for a pensive pause.

"Well?" said the King.

"Are you ready?"

"I've been ready since the liquor ran out!"

"Excellent. In that case, I have a simple query for you, Your Majesty."

The King squirmed impatiently.

"Have you been to your dungeon lately?"

The question hit the King like a cudgel. He had completely forgotten about his dungeon of prisoners. He shook his head.

"I see. And how many captives reside there?"

"There must be several hundred."

"Just as I supposed," said the Wisest Man Alive. "And, unless I miss my guess, I'll bet they're all very hungry, and *very* angry." He coughed. "You must release them."

"I must *what?*"

"Release them."

"They'll tear me apart!"

"Possible."

"So?"

"So you must channel their wrath in the right direction."

"And what direction is that!" the King shouted.

"The direction of the invading army."

"Ah," the King said. He was beginning to understand.

"If the right facts are made evident to your prisoners," his host continued, "they will do whatever you wish. Your captives will clash with General Percy's forces, and the two will cancel each other out."

"You mean they'll kill each other off?"

"I don't like to put it so crassly." The Wisest Man Alive bent toward the King. "Here is what you must do..."

*

Donning the hideous dress a second time, the King made his way through the opposing army—ignoring their lewd remarks—and back into the castle. He crept furtively to his bedchambers and shed the garment.

"I delivered your message to Sir Forsythe," Eliza told him when he entered the throne room. Before leaving, the King had asked her to carry a plea for help to the knight. "He says he would be happy to provide aid, except he's otherwise detained. The demand for a doctor/anatomist has soared since the occupying army arrived and started razing things. He's completely booked."

"It doesn't matter. We don't need him."

"We don't?" Eliza seemed doubtful.

"Ah, ye of little faith. Get the fiddler: we're going to the dungeon."

Eliza knew better than to question the King when he got like this.

By torchlight, the quaint little love triangle descended together through dank passages and narrow stairways. Only the King seemed at all enthusiastic about the venture, pressing ahead and whistling discordantly. Eliza and Frederick lagged behind, and when the fiddler groped through the dark for her hand, Eliza could only allow it.

"Here we are!" the King said cheerfully. They'd arrived at the dungeon. He hefted his torch, producing a chorus of agonized moaning. Once everyone's eyes adjusted to the light, so alien in these dingy recesses, both parties took to studying one another.

The dungeon consisted of a single cavernous room, bordered by hundreds of cells. It was constructed in this way so a ruler would only have to announce once such things as reduced sentences, or—as was more often the case—extended sentences. The King now intended to use this architectural quirk to realize the counsel of the Wisest Man Alive and, fortune permitting, end a siege.

The occupants of the cells themselves looked anything but robust. They were whitish and scrawny. That they hadn't eaten in weeks was painfully evident, except for some, who—

The King frowned. "There are considerably fewer of you," he said, his voice echoing around the prison.

It was true. Many cells contained only one inmate, though they should all have contained two. Even more perplexing: those who lacked cellmates seemed much more fleshed out than the other prisoners. It was almost as if...

"Gods have mercy," the King gasped. Similarly sharp inhalations from Frederick and Eliza told him they had arrived at the same conclusion.

He began his address. "Um, hello," he said loudly. His voice bounced back to him, punctuating his uncertainty. "I see some of you have eaten your cellmates." He coughed. "I'm going to overlook that."

"We wouldn't have done it if Igor was here to feed us!" shouted one vigorous-looking man. Igor was normally responsible for feeding the inmates. "Where's Igor?"

"I gave him a holiday. Listen, it's a long story."

The prisoners all screamed in outrage.

"Be quiet!" the King roared. "Quiet or no one goes free!"

At the word 'free', a respectful silence descended.

"Thank you. Now, hear this: an army of well-trained soldiers has had this castle surrounded for the past month." The King cleared his throat. "I need you to get rid of them for me."

"Bloody likely!" a woman with an eye patch screamed.

"I wouldn't fight a toothless gaffer for you!" another captive shrieked.

"I know some of you may not be altogether fond of me," the King said over the tumult. Their voices rose in agreement. "However!" he yelled. This was where the instructions of the Wisest Man Alive came in. "However. You all have two options. You can either persist in your vendetta against me—and even kill me, when given the chance—or you can listen to what I have to say.

"Oh, and I should mention the latter option involves food."

Their ears perked up.

"I won't lie. There aren't any victuals to be had in the castle. My associates and I have gone hungry for some time. The invading army, however, possesses food in revolting quantities. As we starve inside these stone walls, they gorge excessively on stolen meats. And vegetables, and cheesecakes, and what have you.

"I am going to set you all free now, two by two—or two by one, as the case may be. After that, the choice is yours. I will have no control over your actions."

He turned to Eliza. "Keys."

They approached the first cell. When they entered the view of the occupants, the King gave a start. "Georgianna!" he said in a strangled voice. "It's been a while."

Inside, an attractive young woman glared out at him.

"Who's Georgianna, Your Majesty?" Eliza asked. Her voice had a keenly jealous edge. Frederick eyed her askance.

"She's, uh, just this girl I ate supper with once." He turned back to the cell. "Listen, Georgianna I'm really sorry for—"

"It's okay, sire. Really. For the first three months I was pretty ticked off, but then I fell in love." She gestured tenderly to her cellmate. He waved. "His name is Roberto."

"Hello, Your Majesty," Roberto said brightly. "You sentenced me to life imprisonment for loitering in the Royal Square—remember?"

"Oh, yes," said the King. Perhaps this would prove more tedious than he'd anticipated. "Such fond memories."

He unlocked their cell. They didn't tear him to bits. Instead, they proceeded to the middle of the giant chamber, and waited for him to release the others.

He moved on to the next cell, where the elderly inmate addressed him stridently.

"Making speeches again, are you, boy?" she said in a voice like rusty hinges, clutching the bars. "More like blowing hot air, if you ask me. 'His Royal Highness' my pimply bottom."

"Hello, Mother," the King muttered.

"*Mother?*" Eliza said.

"You locked your own mother in the dungeon?" said Frederick.

"Not a good time, guys," the King said under his breath.

"Of course he locked me in his dungeon!" the old woman crowed, and the King cringed. "He couldn't handle being wrong all the time, that's all!" She hooted with laughter. "Stupid, spoilt boy!"

"Where's your cellmate, Mother?"

"Oh, him? Had to eat him." She pointed to a pile of dusty bones in the corner of her cell. "A shame, too—he was such a nice fellow. Tavern brawler." She pointed a gnarled finger at the King. "See what you drive me to, son?"

The King unlocked and opened the cell. "Please just go wait in the center of the room."

"Wait in the center of the room, he says! After two years of waiting in his dungeon, he tells me to wait in the center of the room!" She cuffed the King on his ear. "You never did have any tact," she cawed up at him, and marched over to join Georgianna and Roberto.

80

The King fingered his ear tenderly. "I hope General Percy gets her."

His army was growing.

They went from cell to cell, releasing prisoners and praying they wouldn't attack. Many prisoners chose to share the crimes for which they'd been imprisoned. After hearing the many reasons the King found for locking folks away, Frederick and Eliza marvelled they weren't prisoners themselves.

Finally all the cells were opened, and the giant chamber packed with freed prisoners. The King said nothing, knowing the time for words had passed. For a protracted moment the mob seemed to teeter between charging up the stairs and lynching the King.

At last, they arrived at a decision. The castle rumbled with their passage.

The King, Frederick and Eliza now stood alone in the empty dungeon. The latter pair seemed both impressed with the King's accomplishment and repelled by his treatment of his mother.

"You've never lived with her," he said. "Now, let's get a good view of the battle."

*

Night had descended, and the only warning had by General Percy's sleeping army was the silent, inexorable lowering of the drawbridge. After a month of inactivity, the soldiers had grown accustomed to two things: gluttony, and sweating in their pitch-black uniforms. The last thing they expected was to be ambushed by hundreds of raging men and women from inside the castle they presumed nearly empty.

High above, from the window of the King's bedchambers, Frederick, Eliza and the King enjoyed an aerial view of the short battle. They watched with an electrifying trepidation as the former prisoners engaged the first rows of sleeping soldiers. Perhaps 'engaged' is too balanced a term, however—what they did was steal their weapons and butcher them in their sleep. Eliza whimpered in horror; Frederick struggled not to throw up. The King thought about how long it had been since he last hunted elk in the nearby wood. That would be the first thing *he* did with his rediscovered freedom.

There are many factors that decide a battle's outcome, however only a few of then have any noticeable effect. Battles are influenced by things like which side is better armed, and which side possesses the element of surprise. But most of all, they are determined by which side is angrier. In this respect, the former inmates were leagues ahead. The conflict ended in minutes, with General Percy and his remaining men scattering in all eight compass directions. Frenzied, the newly liberated convicts harried them through the streets. The King was convinced he spotted his mother at their head, screaming and waving a scimitar.

"We're free," the King declared wonderingly. "And you have the Wisest Man Alive to thank."

Frederick shot him a strange look. "That's a little pretentious, isn't it? I mean, you did well, but I wouldn't say—"

Eliza shushed him. For some reason, she seemed uncomfortable at the mention of her therapist.

The King threw open the window and inhaled the sweet summer air. "Finally free," he murmured. "And it's a beautiful day for hunting."

Suddenly, it began to rain.

"Bugger."

They looked upon the hundreds of bloodied corpses scattered outside. The King whistled. "Who's going to clean up that mess?"

His gaze wandered in the fiddler's direction.

*

The hunting party wound through the town, the King humming happily at its head. They had gone despite the rain, and were rewarded: laid out on litters were three large, healthy stags.

Well, they had been healthy when they were alive.

As they passed the team labouring to clear the ground surrounding the castle, Frederick looked up from his work and glared at the King. The King smiled and flashed him a thumbs-up.

Initially, the fiddler had been alone in the colossal, thankless task of burying the battle's dead. Not one member of the King's former staff had returned. Eventually the King got around to threatening some peasants with execution, thereby filling around half the empty positions. He set ten of them to cleaning up bodies, and now the effort continued apace.

The stable master had been fired immediately after being found in the moat, where he leaped to escape the raging convicts. The King couldn't find a replacement anywhere, and all the horses had to be sold—regrettable, since they'd finally recovered from their bout of colic. The King kept his goat, and took to feeding and watering it. He had a few painful mishaps, but quickly became deft at avoiding its horns.

After releasing a dungeon-load of prisoners, the King had worried his Kingdom's crime rate would skyrocket. It soon became apparent he fretted unnecessarily, however—the convicts either left the Kingdom or remained and behaved themselves. It stood to reason, considering most of them had been imprisoned for abusing the King's patience rather than any actual laws.

He had yet to hear from his mother, and dreaded the day he did.

The King moved quickly through the castle, seeking Eliza. Torn between her boyfriend and the monarch, she continued seeing the Wisest Man Alive regularly, and was given to being absent more often than not.

He found her in the throne room, reclining in his throne. He didn't mind.

"How was the hunt, Your Majesty?"

The King beheld her before answering. She was so beautiful.

"Your Majesty?"

The King gave a small start. "Oh, splendid. Three stags were shot. I pointed the second one out to the archers myself."

"Congratulations," she said, though her voice lacked lustre.

The King frowned, moving closer. Eliza had been despondent ever since the siege lifted. The anxiety of indecision was beginning to overwhelm her.

"I went to the market before coming back," the King said softly. "I bought you something I hope will ease your pain." Tenderly, he rested his hand on her shoulder. "And your decision."

He withdrew a small, elongated box from his pocket. He placed it carefully in her hands.

She opened it. Inside lay a dazzling necklace, studded copiously with diamonds. Eliza held it up to the light cast by the throne room's broken window.

"It's pretty."

The King drew a breath. "Eliza, I'm asking you to leave Frederick and be with me. We mustn't ignore our feelings any longer."

She gazed up at him woefully. "But Your Highness, he's your fiddler!"

"Yes, and a rather good one, at that. But if he should choose to quit, then I shall have to do without. Music is as nothing, compared with the prospect of spending life with you."

Eliza shook her head. "I can't accept this gift, sire. I can't leave Frederick—it would cause him such grief. I'm sorry." She fled the throne room, leaving the necklace behind.

The King stood before his throne, trembling. Abruptly he seized the trinket and hurled it at the smashed-out window through which General Percy's spies had gained entry. It caught on a shard of glass and hung there, glittering like a thousand suns.

*

The man responsible for the King's misery stood obliviously before him and played the fiddle. That he had done nothing wrong, and was in reality a decent fellow, merely further inflamed the King's ire.

A week had passed since the cleanup finished, and Frederick only yesterday returned to being on speaking terms with the King. For days he had refused to play the fiddle, instead choosing to stay locked in his room making dark declarations. His reclusive hiatus allowed Eliza to resume fooling around with the King, which, despite having refused his offer, she did.

The King's options were dwindling rapidly. In fact, there remained only one. Given that Eliza's infernal empathy prevented her from leaving the fiddler, and given that the Wisest Man Alive had refused to compromise his practice, the King was forced to take action he had thus far hesitated to take. Frederick had to be removed.

It was not integrity that, until now, stayed his hand. The King wasn't above ordering a man killed on a whim. It was just that he doubted Eliza, who feared mortally for Frederick's ability to compose music, would appreciate his sudden extermination.

"They've cancelled my subscription to the Kingdom Crier," said Frederick, jolting the King from his sinister reverie. The fiddler was taking a break from fiddling.

"Is that so?" the King said uneasily. He had completely forgotten the Kingdom Crier had printed articles about his affair with Eliza. Had Frederick seen them?

"Yes, it is. I haven't received an issue since before the invaders arrived. They sent me a letter saying my payment was late, though I'm certain I gave them it."

"Couldn't you just pick one up at the market?" said Eliza, who sat nearby.

The King gestured covertly for her to shut up.

"It's the principle of the thing, Alice," Frederick went on. "If they refuse to behave like adults, then I certainly won't buy their silly paper."

The King slumped in his throne, relieved. Evidently Duke Edward thought it would be bad for business if Frederick were to discover about the King and Eliza. The fiddler might put the whole charade to an end, and then the Crier would be forced to find another scandal to leech dry.

Frederick began to play once more, and the King returned to contemplating Frederick's death. It would have to be subtle. It would have to be devious. It would have to be painstakingly calculated, with every kink worked out, every—

A string on Frederick's fiddle snapped, whipping him across the face and eliciting a yelp. The King looked up with interest, but it appeared the fiddler survived.

"Not to worry," Frederick assured them. "I have a second fiddle."

There was a tense pause.

"What did you just say?" the King asked slowly.

Frederick looked up. "I said I brought another. I have a second fiddle."

His latter two words reverberated ominously around the chamber. Finally the echo dispersed, along with the King's self-control.

*

The King fumbled nervously with the contraption he had been provided with. He knew it was called a 'bow', but other than that its use remained a mystery. At his feet lay a 'quiver' of 'arrows'. The King knew he was supposed to combine these instruments in some exotic way, yet so far no one had quite informed him how.

Silently, he mourned subtlety and caution.

Nearby, Frederick handled his bow masterfully. He ran his fingers along its string, checking for something or other. He flexed the bow a few times to gauge its ability to...to do whatever it did. He studied his collection of arrows and, with an expert's eye, selected a promising shaft.

"How is it you're so familiar with bow and arrow, but completely useless with a crossbow?" the King said.

Frederick's reply was smouldering. "They're two completely different things."

The reason Frederick and the King stood on this open field, with a large audience looking on, was simple. After hearing Frederick innocently utter the two words that perfectly characterized the King's plight, the King snapped. In his mad rage, he had challenged the fiddler to a contest of his naming. The loser was to be executed.

Once the initial shock of the proposal passed, Frederick's reply was brief: "Archery."

And now, the King was poised to die by his own royal decree. Desperately he scanned the crowd for aid of any kind. He found only half-hidden snickering at his incompetence.

He resumed his frantic study of the equipment assembled before him. He thought he understood how the quiver and bow were used, but where in the gods' creation did arrows figure in?

Presently the overseer of the event began to speak in ominous tones. "In accordance with ancient custom, the Challenged will be allowed first shot. The Challenger will shoot second. The object is to hit the 'X'." He indicated a white target at the end of the field which, as promised, bore a red 'X' at its center. "One shot only will be allowed per archer. No retakes. No practice shots. And don't try to claim the wind changed, because I've had it up to here with that excuse." The overseer indicated a point far above his head. "Are the contenders ready?"

Frederick nodded confidently. The King tried not to wet himself.

"Very well. Challenged, at your leisure."

The crowd ceased its tittering as Frederick smoothly nocked an arrow and drew the fletching to his cheek. He released. The crowd entered a frenzy of cheering.

The King gaped at the white target. The tiny 'X' was now hidden by the still-quivering shaft.

"Challenger," the overseer intoned, and the crowd fell silent once more. "At your leisure."

The King knew his arrow stood no chance of even reaching the target, let alone hitting it. He also knew either he or Frederick would end this contest dead. At the moment, the King seemed the likely candidate.

Trembling, the King nocked an arrow. It waggled uncertainly in his shaking grasp. The crowd again began to laugh.

He swung the bow around, and aimed it at Frederick.

The crowd gasped.

His bow twanged and the arrow sailed through the air, lodging in the ground pathetically short of the fiddler.

Immediately the overseer piped up. "The contest has run its course. The victor shall depart the field unscathed." He paused. "The defeated shall never leave."

Another man walked onto the field. His black outfit did nothing to hide his muscular frame, and his gait spoke of a man who had flirted with death and come away without any communicable diseases. It was the King's own royal executioner.

The executioner was a fearsome man. Most hangmen choose to remain anonymous, not wishing to be publicly associated with all things morbid. The King's executioner, however, divulged his name freely. It was Earl.

Earl took off his executioner's hood and waved it at the throng, just to show he wore it merely for decorum. The crowd cheered raucously.

Royal decree or no, the King dashed in the opposite direction. He tripped. Within seconds, his employee stood over him. The King lay there, trembling, overwhelmed by Earl's imposing presence.

The executioner produced a small, concealable axe. "For last-minute appointments," he said. "I'm sorry about this, boss. You've really helped me along with my career." He raised the axe overhead.

"Stop!" a reedy voice cried. "No one has to die!"

The executioner lowered the axe and studied his nails.

The King stood and quickly distanced himself from the gleaming blade.

The voice belonged to the Wisest Man Alive, who strode purposefully across the field, his beard fluttering dramatically. The King had never felt such affection for another human being. Which was somewhat ironic, as very shortly he would loathe the old man utterly.

"Though it may not be known to all parties," the Wisest Man Alive said, "the true prize of this contest is not survival, but the heart of a young maiden. You see, His Majesty issued his challenge in order to eliminate Frederick, so that he might have this maiden to himself. It is a forgivable oversight that His Highness failed to consider he possesses no special talent in…well, anything."

The King frowned.

"But I digress. What I am here to say is this contest need not have taken place, for the young maiden in question is no longer available to be won."

Suddenly the crowd parted, and Eliza joined the others on the field. Frederick looked at her questioningly.

"What is he talking about, Alice?" the fiddler said.

"Frederick, I'm so sorry." Eliza averted her gaze. "I haven't been completely faithful."

"That's right!" the King said. He rounded on Frederick with a fierce grin. "She's in love with me!"

At his words Eliza started, growing more remorseful by the second. "Actually, I haven't been very honest with you either, Your Majesty."

The King gaped. "What?"

"Allow me to elucidate," said the Wisest Man Alive. "Alice—or Eliza, as the King tends to call her—loves neither Frederick nor His Excellence. She's in love with…"

…the crowd shivered with anticipation…

"…me."

And, in the total silence that followed, Eliza and the Wisest Man Alive shared a lengthy, passionate kiss.

The overseer, who till now had maintained admirable composure, retched violently. Not only was the man Eliza kissed the Wisest Alive, but he was probably also the Oldest.

The day's drama having passed, the crowd departed. A reporter for the Kingdom Crier could be seen scribbling furiously in his notebook. Anyone in the Kingdom not present to witness these events would learn of them, in exaggerated detail, the following morning.

Eliza and the Wisest Man Alive continued to kiss noisily. Frederick, the overseer, the executioner and the King all shared awkward glances. They too left the archery field in short order.

*

Frederick and the King sat side by side at the tavern's bar, staring into their respective drinks. They didn't speak. Things were a little strained between them.

At a nearby table, some men were carousing loudly, drinking and jostling each other in manly fashion.

"I was at the archery field today," one burly man announced. "What entertainment!"

"I heard about that," another said. "Didn't the King almost lose his head?"

Apparently they hadn't noticed Fredrick and the King.

"He might as well have lost it," a third piped up. "He lost near everything else."

"Aye," said the first man. "The contest, his woman and his dignity."

"Hasn't had much luck lately, our King, has he? First he's in the papers, then he's under siege, and now this! Next his castle will burn down, just like the last King, and that'll be that."

The King frowned.

"And the fiddler! Who'd of thought a scrawny bard like that could ever fire a bow?"

They all laughed.

The King and Frederick shared a pained glance. As one, they took a long draught from their mugs.

"I," said Frederick, when he finally set down his drink, "place complete blame with you. For everything."

"That," said the King, "is perfectly understandable."

For a long while, they said nothing.

Frederick spoke again. "I still need a job."

"And I a fiddler."

They continued to gaze into their ale long into the night.

THE END.

K
♠

The King
of
Spades

♠
K

Frederick's eyes were filled with remorse. This was especially noteworthy, since for Frederick to look at the King with anything other than murderous intent was rare.

"There's something I need to get off my chest," the fiddler rasped, as if on the verge of tears. "I—I killed."

The King cleared his throat. "You killed? That sentence requires an object to be of any use to me. Who did you kill?"

"I killed a man."

"Okay. That eliminates half the population. Which one?"

Frederick's answer, and its immediate repercussions, changed everything. It dethroned the King, for one—but this only surprised him because it hadn't happened sooner.

THE END.

The word 'king' can be given a myriad of definitions, however the most widely accepted seems to be "person responsible for the wellbeing of a large number of other people."

Our King wasn't much for the wellbeing of others, nor was he very responsible. That he lay facedown in a poorly maintained, mud-filled road, and that passersby kicked him and cursed his mother, only served to emphasize this fact.

This didn't really concern the King. What presently concerned him was suicide, and what it might do to improve his miserable existence. Death, he'd decided, was the only answer to life's futility.

Unfortunately, it seemed death was also futile—a conclusion encouraged by the presence of the King's advisor, who, only minutes ago, the King would have sworn deceased.

Minutes ago was when the apparently reincarnated advisor made his appearance. The King was minding his own business (brooding) when someone shouted angrily at him. He lifted his head from the mud without much enthusiasm, and saw a horse-drawn wagon hurtling toward him through the rain. He replaced his head. It was a fitting death.

Suddenly the horses reared up, eyes rolling fearfully, and the wagon halted. Peasants began to scream, scattering in all directions. The street quickly emptied.

In the ensuing silence, something behind the King squelched inexorably toward him.

Sufficiently motivated, the King rolled over to behold a monstrosity, which was covered in soil and had a wicked fracture splitting its cranium. The brains remaining inside jiggled as the thing walked.

The abomination stopped within inches of the King. "Good morshgul, sire," it said cheerfully.

The King gaped in utter horror. And, having rediscovered his will to live, he fled.

*

The King trudged back to his castle, the leafy trees a fiery nimbus surrounding him. It was autumn again, and like last year, his heart was shattered. He drank, and he pined, and he bided his time. Above all, he neglected his duties.

It had been twelve months since he lay shirtless atop Devil's Drop. Since then, he had gotten nowhere.

When he returned to the castle, a peasant wearing a wide-brimmed hat lingered near the drawbridge. The headwear cast his face in shadow, with only his mouth visible as he addressed the muddied monarch:

"Why, sire, whatever has happened? You're a mess!"

The King gritted his teeth. "I am in possession of both an empty dungeon and little respect for idle paupers. Do not try my benevolence."

Encounters with the undead made the King slightly irritable.

"I apologize in advance, Your Majesty, however my humble lexicon is insufficient to accommodate your rather substantial one. If you would kindly moderate your verbosity and speak at a more provincial level, I would be much obliged."

The King stared at the peasant. At length he bent down to study the man's face. "Sir Forsythe, is that you?"

The doctor, alchemist, knight and—most recently—anatomist took off his hat and stared into it, embarrassed. "It is I, my liege."

"Why are you in disguise?"

"In truth, I wear this hat because I am ashamed. You might say it is the hat of shame."

"But what are you ashamed of?"

"I have been a bad friend."

"To whom?"

"To you, sire!"

The King, who had not been aware he had a friend, was not too put off.

Sir Forsythe elaborated: "I failed to lend aid in your time of need."

The King waved the confession away. "There's nothing you could have done about Eliza."

"I refer to the siege, Your Majesty."

The King frowned. "Oh, that. Yes, well, that was rather another matter."

The knight hung his head. He began to put the hat back on.

The King, with sudden inspiration, said, "Give me that hat." Sir Forsythe hesitantly complied.

The King flung it into the moat. It sank. "Be ashamed no more, noble Forsythe!"

"That was my favourite hat!"

"But I thought you said—"

"It wasn't *really* the hat of shame! I was speaking figuratively!"

The King shrugged. "The man-eating alligators have it now."

"Are there man-eating alligators in your moat?"

"No."

Forsythe gazed forlornly into the moat. He seemed to consider jumping in after it. He sighed. "I suppose I deserved that."

The King nodded. "Yes. You did. Would you like to come inside?"

Sir Forsythe accepted the invitation, and they crossed the drawbridge to the castle. On their way through the entrance foyer, the King picked up the copy of the Kingdom Crier that awaited him. Duke Edward now personally ensured it was delivered to his castle daily.

He read today's headline. 'HIS EXCELLENCE SIGHTED LYING FACEDOWN IN MUD! SOURCES SAY HE CAN ONLY GO UP FROM HERE.'

"My, but they're getting good," the King murmured.

As they reached the dining chamber, Sir Forsythe gestured toward the newspaper. "What's that, Your Highness?"

The King looked up in disbelief. "Why, this is the Kingdom Crier."

"Oh. I think I've heard of it. Quite respectable, isn't it?"

The King frowned as he poured Forsythe a glass of mead. "Haven't you read it?"

Forsythe shook his head. "No time," he said. He looked at the headline. "That's a little untoward, isn't it?"

Wordlessly, the King walked to a nearby end table and returned with several past issues. He set them before the knight. "Peruse these."

Sir Forsythe flipped through them, his consternation growing. "But this is dishonourable!"

"To put it mildly, yes."

"This is utter filth! Why don't you exile these vile parasites?"

"I've tried. Several times."

Sir Forsythe leaped suddenly from his seat, hand on sword hilt. "Your Majesty, I may have been absent during the siege, but today, I atone. By sunset, this blight will be purged from the land. I give my word."

His guest's vigour excited the King tremendously. He was unused to anybody siding with him. He drew himself up, regarding Forsythe momentously. "Kneel," he commanded.

Unsure, Forsythe knelt.

The King took his guest's sword and pressed its flat edge to both of Forsythe's shoulders, and then to his head. "With the power vested in me, I hereby knight thee."

"Er, Your Majesty?"

"Yes, Sir Forsythe?"

"I was already a knight."

The King blinked. "Ah. Right. Well in that case, rise and go forth, loyal creature!"

Forsythe rose, dusting himself off. He decided to overlook the King's obscene breech of protocol. He cleared his throat. "Where are the stables, Your Majesty? I require a steed."

The King hesitated. "What sort of steed?"

"A noble one, preferably."

"How about a goat?"

The knight sighed. This was very anticlimactic. "Can you hand me another issue of the Crier?"

"Why?"

"I need to rekindle my ire."

The King did as he asked.

With one glance, Sir Forsythe turned red with outrage. "Faw! Such disgraceful refuse should never have been committed to papyrus!" He turned to the King. "We ride!"

They headed for the stables, and when their progress was impeded by the door that lacked a doorknob, Sir Forsythe simply kicked it open. Their entrance provoked a cacophony of enraged bleating. After months of inactivity the King's goat had become a raging beast, given to frothing at the mouth and skewering anyone foolish enough to draw near. Now it waited in its corner stall and bleated death threats.

"How long since this animal was last ridden?" asked Sir Forsythe.

"Over a year."

Sir Forsythe spread his feet to steady himself. "Open the stall door."

The King did so, keeping safely out of the goat's path.

The goat charged at the knight with berserker speed. In its wrath, the King saw the ruination of their fledgling plan. No man could survive a charge like that. The King would never defeat Duke Edward.

Forsythe met the goat halfway, grabbing its horns and forcing its head back. They grappled for a few tense seconds, until at last their struggle ended with the goat pinned on its back. It bleated wearily.

The knight stood up, releasing it. The goat awkwardly righted itself, and regarded Forsythe deferentially. The King gaped. Sir Forsythe had earned the goat's respect.

"You are a remarkable man," he said. His guest waved the compliment away.

The King rode sitting behind the knight, and enjoyed an astonishingly smooth ride. The goat responded fluidly to the knight's prompting. Their enterprise had barely begun, and already Sir Forsythe had accomplished the impossible.

"We repair briefly to my hovel," the knight said. "There are items I must fetch."

In the front room of Sir Forsythe's cottage, an adolescent boy awaited them. It seemed he was trying to imitate the knight's facial hair, with little success.

"I thought I told you to shave," said Forsythe. He turned to the King. "Your Majesty, this is my page. Incidentally, he is also my nurse, my apprentice potion maker and my surgical assistant. Come, boy. I prepare for battle."

Forsythe and his page retired to the rear of the house, while the King waited out front. He waited a ridiculously long time.

Wandering around the front room of Sir Forsythe's modest home, the King beheld many strange things. There were several objects that appeared to be in various stages of creation. The King hoped their purpose would be more apparent when they were completed.

Posted near the door he found a short poem—a haiku. He was shocked to discover himself listed as the author.

"Sorry, sire," Sir Forsythe said upon returning. "Donning armour takes so dreadfully long. Safety first, though." The knight wore a crimson tunic over his chain mail. A line of oblong bumps formed a peculiar impression across his middle, but the King was too impatient to inquire.

They embarked for the Kingdom Crier, renewing their fury en route with copies they'd brought for that purpose.

The offices of the Crier loomed before them, eight floors and countless dishonest stories high. They dismounted, and Forsythe tied the goat to a post using a slipknot. "We'll have to depart quickly," he said.

An autumn wind blew, eliciting a seasonal comment from the quixotic warrior. "Harvest time is upon us." Forsythe drew his sword. "Let us reap."

He charged through the entranceway.

The King shrugged, and followed at a safe distance.

Inside, Sir Forsythe held the receptionist at sword point. Her usual condescending smile was now a fearful grimace.

The knight spoke in a guttural growl. "The only reason I don't slay you, hell-demon, is because you were cunning enough to take a female form. Kindly leave with your life, lest my mind changes."

The receptionist, shedding all pretensions, scampered over the desk and out the door.

"Lead on!" the knight urged the King.

The King shook his head and pointed at the stairs. "The editor works on the seventh floor. You lead on."

For the third and hopefully final time, the King entered the cavernous hallway leading to Duke Edward's office. As they dashed along its length, he thought of all the unpleasant memories created behind those double doors. In that office he had faced his advisor's betrayal, confessed to inferior intelligence, and donned a woman's dress. It was satisfying to hear the sound of splintering oak when the knight booted open the doors.

Duke Edward sat working at his desk. He looked up and grinned, as though his office doors hadn't just been kicked in. "Visitors! A welcome distraction from the tedium of my work. Even with a monarch like ours, for quality smut one must dig deep. How may I help you?"

"We have come to exterminate you," Sir Forsythe said.

"Yeah!" the King said, unable to contain his exuberance.

"Sir Forsythe, I'm stunned—primarily because you arrive in such poor company, but also your harsh words. Has the Kingdom Crier ever wronged you?"

"Your very existence wrongs my *soul*."

Duke Edward nodded vigorously. "Yes, that's the whole idea!"

The knight levelled his blade, approaching slowly. "Enough talk."

The editor reached into his desk, and suddenly Sir Forsythe found a crossbow aimed at his heart. Duke Edward smiled. "It's unfortunate I have to kill you, oh righteous knight. I'm a great admirer of alchemy." He paused. "And of medicine, anatomy and knighthood. But you insist on being removed."

The crossbow fired, the bolt bouncing harmlessly off Sir Forsythe's armour.

Duke Edward frowned. Then he bent under his oaken desk and rose clutching an enormous halberd, adorned excessively with golden scrollwork and endowed with a wicked blade.

"Are you compensating for something?" Sir Forsythe said.

Remaining grimly silent, the Duke circled the desk and squared off with his adversary.

The King cowered behind a marble statue.

It is illustrative of Sir Forsythe's high nobility that the finest thing Duke Edward ever did was perish by the knight's sword. Or perhaps it is illustrative of what a lamentable person the Editor was. At any rate, though skilled in combat, Duke Edward only managed to parry two of Sir Forsythe's blows before losing his head. Literally.

The King looked on in fearful awe as Sir Forsythe made strangers of the Editor's head and neck. The former hit the floor with a terse *thud,* and stared up at the King, expressionless. Even in death, Duke Edward remained insufferably cool.

Forsythe stripped off his tunic, revealing a row of red cylinders strapped to his breastplate.

"What's that?" the King asked, marvelling at this strange, fearsome man.

"Dynamite. A recent invention of mine."

"What does it do?"

The alchemist in Sir Forsythe smiled devilishly. "I don't completely know. But I can almost assure you these offices won't be standing in another ten minutes."

It was the best thing the King had heard all week.

The knight produced flint and steel, lighting the lengthy fuse that protruded from the cylinders. It sparkled merrily.

"Now what?" said the King.

"We run."

And that's what they did. They sped from the office as though chased by lions. Their progress, however, was impeded by five reporters, who waited in the hall brandishing maces, daggers, and in one case, a stapler.

"This is an outrage!" one shouted. "What about freedom of speech?"

"You're free to speak your last words," Forsythe said.

Battle was joined. For his part, the King ducked back inside the office and egged Forsythe on from just inside the entrance. As for the reporters—well, they died.

The victors were about to leave when they heard a doleful whining coming from a previously unnoticed doorway. Inside, they found a woman chained to a desk. The desk bore a plaque: "Countess Francine, Indisposed Journalist."

"Who are you?" asked the King redundantly.

"Can't you read? I'm Francine. Are you going to make me write another story?"

"No," Forsythe replied. "We're going to blow this place up."

Francine brightened.

"How long have you been chained to that desk?" said the King, making conversation.

"Going on two years, now. It started when they found out I'm good with a pen. They needed someone to write articles for them, and so they snatched me up overnight and brought me here." She paused. "I really mean 'overnight', you know—they took me from my house at two in the morning."

Sir Forsythe fell to his knees in dismay. "They forced you to write for this vile publication? Oh angel, how your purity is tainted!"

"Didn't your neighbours notice you were gone?" asked the King.

"Oh, no. No one misses a Countess. I mean, if a Duke gets misplaced, everyone panics. Knights, too—whole Kingdom up in arms. Even Counts receive some notice. But Countesses? Ha! You're lucky if they bother to presume you dead. Often they won't, and then you don't even get an obituary. I'm sure *I* didn't, and I would know."

Sir Forsythe could take no more. He dashed around the desk and began hacking at the Countess' chains with his sword. Sparks flew, but little headway was made.

The knight stood upright, wiping sweat from his brow. "Your Majesty, it's futile! The fuse grows short, but these chains are too strong for even Edwardslayer!"

"Edwardslayer?"

The knight shrugged. "My sword needs a name. I thought I'd try it out."

"Well, can't you disable the fuse?"

"I could, however I doubt we'd ever get this opportunity again. The time for action is now!"

The King considered briefly. "Leave her."

Forsythe shook his head. "It's against my moral code, sire."

"To hell with your moral code! Can't you make an exception?"

"Exceptions are also against my moral code."

The King strained desperately for a solution. His eyes fell on the chain. "Wait—isn't that merely shackled to the desk's leg? Can't we just lift the desk?"

Sir Forsythe quickly assessed the situation. "Brilliant!" he said. Together, he and the King attempted to pick up the massive writing table.

They gave up. "No use," the knight panted. "It's made of iron-wood."

"Can I help?" said Francine.

Forsythe waved her away. "Spare your delicate arms."

She gripped the desk's bottom edge. "I prefer to spare the rest of my body. Heave!"

Together, they raised the desk enough to kick the shackle out from under it.

Forsythe stared at her, impressed.

Francine grinned. "I really hate this place."

The three of them dashed down the stairs, Countess Francine's chain bouncing crazily behind them. Outside, the goat bleated. They all scrambled to get on top of it, with the King practically hanging from the rear. "Forward!" Forsythe commanded, booting the animal's flanks.

The goat remained motionless, bleating stubbornly.

"*Forward!*" the knight insisted.

The goat pawed the ground.

"*Go, you filthy, flea-infested—*"

Suddenly one of two things happened, but from that day forth the King was never able to decide which. Either sound disappeared altogether, or the world became made of sound. At any rate, he flew through the air and hit the ground with a squelch. For the second time that day he lay facedown in mud, within inches of death.

Little by little the world as he knew it returned, accompanied by an unmentionable amount of pain. Nearby, something cried out weakly. The King crawled toward the pathetic sound.

"Impossible," the King rasped. It was the goat. The bloody thing had survived.

He found both Forsythe and Francine lying in a ditch, in similar health. "Marry me, Sir Forsythe," the Countess was pleading between agonized moans. "You're handsome, you saved my life, and best of all, I've never written an article about you. Please marry me."

The battered knight shook his head woefully. "I'm afraid I must decline, fair maiden." He winced, rubbing his backside. "I'm far too busy for wedlock."

The Countess pouted. "Marriage isn't a chore!"

"Actually," said the King, "I can see his point."

"You stay out of this! I've written plenty of stories about *you*."

Countess Francine would henceforth pester the knight so incessantly they might as well have been married. This was foreshadowed by the fact when the King and Forsythe shook hands and parted ways, Francine followed the wearied knight home.

As for the King, he was physically drained but emotionally vigorous. The Kingdom Crier was no more. Never again would he be accused of putting on a dress, a bonnet or even a garter. He wore a triumphant smile during the entire crawl home.

*

He returned to find his throne room in shambles. Broken bottle shards glittered near his throne, where the drinker of its contents had apparently hurled it. He ducked, and a second bottle whistled overhead, smashing spectacularly behind him. He gulped.

Upon the throne slumped Frederick, clutching his fiddle and glaring. "Good afternoon, Your Despicableness," the fiddler growled. "Finally decided to show your cowardly face, have you?"

"I've been busy."

Roaring drunkenly, Frederick threw his fiddle at the King. Immediately realizing what he'd done, he screeched, "Catch that!"

The King awkwardly intercepted the instrument with his stomach.

Frederick was angry with the King because he blamed him for stealing his girlfriend. The King thought this ridiculous, since he was obviously incapable of such a feat.

He handed the fiddle to its owner, who had sobered considerably. Frederick only had one fiddle left, having thrown the spare at his liege the previous week.

"Did you hear the explosion?" the King said.

Frederick grunted. "I thought you might have something to do with that. Whose dreams have you defiled now?"

"Actually, I did a very fine thing this morning. My greatest accomplishment."

"Greater than forming a coherent sentence?" the fiddler asked. "I find it astounding every time you accomplish that."

"I blew up the offices of the Kingdom Crier."

The fiddler's expression grew solemn. "Well, now, that really is something." He coughed. "You have visitors, by the way. I told them to wait in the dining chamber."

"Visitors?" the King said. He silently vowed that if the blacksmiths had returned, again refusing to forge guillotine blades, he would have the whole ethical lot of them executed. "I'll need my throne, then."

Grumbling, Frederick moved to his usual post, readying his fiddle. Pausing, he asked, "Why are you covered in mud and soot?"

The dramatic arrival of the King's visitors spared him from responding.

Instead of blacksmiths, a group of flamboyantly dressed men and women cart-wheeled through the door. The King sat, dumbstruck, while inside his throne room an extravagant acrobatic performance unfolded. The still drunken Frederick, unsure whether he should play or not, compromised with a slow, mournful tune. The visitors, affected by neither the music nor the throne room's disorderly state, continued to flounce gaily about. Frederick's funeral march plodded on.

Finally the madness ceased, or was at least restrained, long enough for a man sporting a jester's hat and spectacles to approach the King and hand him a business card. He bowed as the King stared at it.

The card read, "The Traveling Linguists' Guild: Performers, Nomads, Field Researchers."

The King, terrified of looking stupid, adopted a knowing expression.

The bespectacled man spoke. "Do you know what Linguistics is, Your Highness?"

The King shook his head knowingly.

The man cleared his throat. "It's the study of language," he said in a rehearsed tone. "Language, you see, is innate—so innate that for a long time, we didn't even notice we were using it. Then some astute individual pointed it out, and that's how Linguistics was born."

His companions beamed and nodded agreement. One did a backflip.

"We," the man continued, "the Traveling Linguists' Guild, travel the world in search of a unified theory of language. We are also acrobats." He paused. "I'm Larry."

The man's speech answered none of the questions cluttering the King's head. In fact, it fostered a few. He asked the most obvious one.

"Yes, but—*why?*" His visitors frowned collectively, and the King elaborated. "I mean, we already have language. It's been invented, and we know how to use it. Why does it merit studying?"

Larry exchanged furtive glances with his colleagues. He cleared his throat several times. He adjusted his jester's hat.

At length he said, "It's very complicated, Your Majesty. I doubt you'd understand."

Frederick, who had stopped playing some time ago, posed a more immediate question. "Why are you here?"

"Ah," the man replied, as though Frederick made some insightful point. "That is why we came." He paused. "To your castle. In order to tell you why, that is." He glanced nervously at the King. "Why we're here."

"Go on," said the King. For someone who studied language, Larry was certainly inept in its usage.

Regaining his composure, Larry continued. "As I said, Your Highness, we travel the world studying various peoples and cultures. Our search for a theory of language has been long and harrowing. However, I am pleased to announce we believe we've finally found one."

He paused, as though expecting something to happen. "So?" said the King.

"We believe we've found one," Larry went on, "that fits the language of every land we've traveled to. Except one."

The King waited.

"It is an unnamed land, filled with oafish savages. Unimportant savages. The language they speak is—well, we find it somewhat irksome. It contains phrases filled only with prepositions. It is comprised of half implosive sounds—sounds involving the intake of air—and half explosive sounds—sounds that involve exhaling. As a result, speakers normally hyperventilate after a few sentences, and then keel over. Their language completely defies our otherwise unified theory."

The King yawned. "I've yet to see how this concerns me."

"Well sire, we've come, your humble supplicants, to ask a small favour. It isn't much of a bother at all, really. We would be very grateful if you'd take the time to—how should I put this—um, exterminate every last one of them. It would work wonders for our theory." Larry smiled.

The King studied the bespectacled man for a long time. "You want me," he said finally, "to execute an entire people? An entire *culture*?"

The whole room held its breath.

"Er, yes, Your Majesty. In essence."

"I see," the King said. "Would you like them beheaded or hanged?"

*

The King couldn't help but smile as the Traveling Linguists' Guild filed out of his throne room. When the last linguist left, the smile became a fit of outright giggling. Frederick, offended by his happiness, stormed off.

This was a day of unprecedented events. Never before had visitors left his throne room feeling at all satisfied. As well, never had his lack of respect for human life been so positively received. People usually found it somewhat abrasive.

Best of all, there was no pesky newspaper around to cast his accomplishments in a negative light.

Something warm welled up in the King—something he couldn't quite name. Anyone else could have told him this was called 'self-respect', and that he had no business feeling it. But the King didn't normally consort with anyone else, and so he remained blissfully ignorant.

"I ought to have a snack," the King said. "A snack, in my honour. I deserve it." And he hurried to his dining chamber, only to find someone already having a snack.

"Who in the gods' respective names are you?" the King roared.

The man sitting at the far end of the table rose regally. In fact, he appeared to do everything regally. He stared regally down his nose at the King. He wore a funny golden hat and a purple robe in a very regal way. "I," he declared regally, "am King Cedric V. Who are you?"

"I'm the King!"

King Cedric studied him for a moment. "*You're* the King?" He paused. "Well, do you have a name?"

"Er, yes."

"What is it?"

"The—King! I'm the King!"

"So you said. But what are you the King *of?*"

"I don't know! The Kingdom! Why, what are *you* the King of?"

King Cedric V drew himself up regally. "I am King and Master of the Northern Realm."

The King blinked. "Where's that?"

"In the north, of course."

The Kings stared at each other across the table for a while, both utterly without anything to say.

"What are you doing in my dining chamber?" the King finally asked.

"I was told to wait here by a man with a fiddle. In the meantime, I am dining."

The King reflected that Frederick *had* informed him of visitors in the dining chamber, but not of a specific number, or nature. He also reflected on whether he really needed a fiddler anyway.

"Why don't you join me?" said King Cedric.

Reluctantly, the King sat. King Cedric snapped his fingers, and a procession of servants wearing chef's hats entered the room. They carried several enticing dishes.

"I don't recall having servants with chef's hats," the King said.

"They're with me, actually. I offer you their services as a token of my gratitude."

"Gratitude for what?" the King asked suspiciously.

"For the hospitality you'll no doubt show me."

The King frowned.

Suddenly, a brightly clad young woman burst into the dining chamber, clearly distressed. Her attire named her a member of the Traveling Linguists' Guild, though the King hadn't noticed her before. Given her striking beauty, he had no idea why not.

"Your Majesty," she said breathlessly. "I need desperately to speak with you concerning your earlier decree."

The King, already in love with the woman, addressed the visiting monarch condescendingly. "As you can see, King Cedric, I have a supplicant to entertain. I frequently entertain supplicants, and my decisions are always well received. Kindly leave. I will deal with you later."

King Cedric smiled. "Nonsense! Here is the perfect opportunity for me to see how business is conducted in this Kingdom. Besides, whatever this young lady has to say, she can say in front of both of us."

The King began to wonder at what point he'd become a guest in his own castle. He turned to the woman and motioned for her to continue.

She cleared her throat. "Well, Your Majesty, I feel I must object to your agreement with the Linguists' Guild. The people they speak of is an intriguing one, and to execute them would be——"

"Excuse me?" King Cedric said. "Did someone say *execute?*"

"Well, yes," said the King. "Execution, you see—very effective instrument, rather a favourite of mine. Er——"

"In the Northern Realm, we haven't put anyone to death for decades! You mean to say you're considering killing off an entire *population?*"

"Oh, he isn't considering it," said the woman.

King Cedric relaxed.

"He's *already* decided to kill off an entire population."

King Cedric rounded on the King.

"There seems to have been a misunderstanding!" the King shouted, making up in loudness what he lacked in logic. "When I said 'execute'—ah—what I really meant was—hmm—I meant bother. Mildly."

His guests studied him in quiet consternation.

As a last resort, he turned to the female linguist. "Would you like to have dinner with me?"

*

"So, uh, what's your name?"

To the King's alarm, the young woman from the Traveling Linguists' Guild had immediately accepted his invitation to dine with him. It was a long time since his last date. Well, admittedly, he had never been on one. Unless you counted Georgianna, and that had ended in disaster. Oh, and Alice. No need to add much there.

At any rate, the King was justifiably nervous, and without any idea of what to say.

"I'm Elizabeth, but you can call me Liz. In fact, if you don't call me Liz, I shall hit you. I hate the name Elizabeth."

"Aha!" the King responded, unable to come up with anything coherent.

A waiter came and took their order. The King asked for a modest plate of roast lamb, but Elizabeth seemed to want everything on the menu, with extra. The King hoped she didn't expect him to pay.

When the waiter finished jotting down Elizabeth's extensive order, he left them staring awkwardly at each other.

"So, what do you do?" the King managed at length.

"I wait for meal."

"No, I mean, what do you—"

"It was a joke."

The King cleared his throat. "Oh. It was funny." He forced a smile.

"I'm a linguist, silly. That's why I'm in the Linguists' Guild."

"Yes, but don't you specialize in anything?"

He soon regretted asking.

Elizabeth's eyes lit up. "Why, yes, actually. I study the communication system of European honeybees—the Italian honeybee, to be specific. Did you know their system is the closest in the animal kingdom to human language?"

The King stared, already dumbfounded by the sheer monotony of the lecture. "Uh, no. I didn't," he said, hoping fervently it wouldn't provoke her to continue.

He hoped in vain. "It's true! Their communication system is capable of producing an infinite number of messages, just like ours! They convey messages through a series of dances: the circle dance, the sickle dance and the tail-wagging dance. The circle dance, used to indicate a food source under twenty meters away, consists of..."

The King shifted uncomfortably. His eyes watered from sheer boredom. He glanced around, desperate for diversion. Elizabeth didn't appear to notice his inattention.

"...and, finally, the tail-wagging dance, which tells of a food source over sixty feet away. The speed of the dance indicates proximity, direction is indicated by the angle of the tail-wagging, and the vigour of the dance indicates the quality of the food source."

The King gazed at her blearily. Could it be? Could she finally be finished talking?

"Well, what do you think?"

The King grimaced, not sure what to say. Finally, though he knew he shouldn't, he said, "But what's the point?"

Elizabeth didn't seem offended. In fact, she bent toward him conspiratorially and said, "I mean to talk with them."

The King nearly choked on a Brussels sprout. "With the honeybees?"

She nodded emphatically. "I've been practising all the dances."

"But—but aren't there obvious proportional difficulties?"

Elizabeth smiled, clearly glad he'd asked. "Well..."

And she began her lecture anew. She talked straight through nine courses, and three deserts. She talked through the waiter's delivery of the bill, and through the King's near fainting spell at the cost there described.

"Well, Your Majesty," she said finally, "It appears we didn't get to discuss your decree. Where does the time go? We'll have to meet again." With that, she bounced out of her seat and departed.

The waiter reappeared, holding out his palm politely yet firmly.

"How can a woman be so beautiful," the King asked him, "and at the same time so completely insufferable?"

The waiter raised his eyebrows. "It's quite common, sire."

*

His spirits heavy and his wallet light, the King retired to his bed-chamber, not bothering to undress. Lying in the dark, he began to reflect on the events of the afternoon and evening, but had to leave off—it was too depressing.

At present he heard raspy breathing coming from nearby. Unless the King completely missed his guess, somebody lay in bed with him. Cautiously, he lit the bedside torch.

He screamed.

There are those one enjoys finding in one's bed, and there are those one does not. The King's undead advisor definitely belonged to the latter category. The pillow on the left side of the bed—king-sized, of course—was now smeared with a pink, organic mush. The advisor grinned with what remained of his face.

"It is quite a nice glarb you have here, Your Jarful!"

The King got out of bed and began inching toward the door, never taking his eyes off of the advisor.

Drawn by the King's scream, King Cedric V burst into the bed-chambers. Accompanying him were two guards who, at seeing the advisor, promptly turned and fled.

"That man needs medical attention!" said King Cedric.

"That man needs to be thrown down a well!" said the King.

But the visiting monarch had already left the chamber again, shouting for medical staff.

"Ha!" the King barked. "He certainly won't find any doctors in this castle."

Five white-clad men bustled in and surrounded the advisor, using several complicated-looking instruments on him. They ignored the King's startled expression. Actually, they ignored him completely.

"Pulse is fine," one observed wonderingly.

"Blood pressure's stable, too," remarked another.

"Who are you people?" the King demanded, having grown tired of being perpetually baffled.

"Why, only the finest doctors in all the Northern Realm!" King Cedric said as he re-entered the room. "You look stressed, Your Highness. Would you like a drink mixed by the finest *barkeeps* in all the—"

"Isn't there anybody left in the Northern Realm?" asked the King. "You must have brought enough people to populate a—a—"

"An entire castle?" King Cedric said. "Really, you shouldn't complain. When I arrived, the only staff I could find was a fiddler, an executioner, and a few guards. Now we have a proper entourage."

"*We?*"

"Er, you." King Cedric smiled.

Presently, the head doctor approached King Cedric. "Sire, the patient's condition is like none we've encountered. After suffering trauma like he's suffered, it's a miracle he survived."

The King cleared his throat. "Er, he didn't."

"Sorry?" said the doctor.

"He didn't survive. He was my advisor, and he died. I witnessed his burial."

"Humour him," whispered King Cedric to the doctor, failing utterly to mask his words.

The doctor nodded. "Of course he did," he said to the King. "The patient died, decided death didn't suit him, and then magically came alive again." He wiggled the fingers of both hands. "Poof!"

Despite the doctor's sarcasm, his depiction of events was uncannily accurate.

"Your Majesty," King Cedric said, "why not entrust your advisor to our care? We will treat him, diagnose his condition, and give you a full report. How does that sound?"

"To be honest," the King said, "I don't give a midden heap what you do with him."

*

If he hadn't spent the rest of the night staring wide-eyed at the ceiling, the King would have been seriously ticked off when Elizabeth flew into his bedchambers shortly before dawn.

"Rise and shine, sire!"

"What are *you* doing here?"

"Why, Your Majesty—we agreed to meet again!"

"It's five AM."

Ignoring this perfectly valid fact, Elizabeth harried him out of his bed (which was cleaned of brains), through the halls and out into the castle gardens. It was raining. The King trudged blearily, fighting to stay awake and dreading another honeybee sermon.

"You simply can't kill off a whole race," Elizabeth said.

The King sighed, relieved they were discussing genocide instead of Italian honeybees.

"Why not?" he said.

"Because it isn't good conduct! You can't just behead whomever you like."

"But I don't behead whomever I like! It's the ones I dislike that get their heads chopped off."

"But that's horrid, Your Highness! Haven't you ever been to an execution?"

The King paused for thought. "As a matter of fact, no, I haven't. Why? Are they any good?"

So it was they decided to attend the public hanging that afternoon. When Elizabeth left to get breakfast, the King began feeling quite contented. He sat down on an ornate concrete bench and watched two birds circle each other playfully.

"And I worried we'd have nowhere to go for our second date!"

*

Aside from Frederick's increasingly discordant music, everything was right with the King. The Kingdom Crier was disbanded and he had rediscovered love, an event he only recently deemed impossible. Certainly, King Cedric was getting a little overbearing, but this was as nothing to someone who had spent childhood with the King's mother—which the King had.

"I'd rather be deaf than hear that trash," he said cheerily to Frederick from his throne.

Frederick stopped, and glared up at him. "Listen, you cretin. My heart is broken, I've been drunk for three weeks, and you haven't paid me in four. What do you expect?"

"You should lighten up."

Frederick started again, this time furiously dragging his bow across the strings without playing any notes.

"I'm going to an execution today!" the King shouted over the cacophony. "Elizabeth is coming!"

Frederick ceased his racket for the second time. "But there isn't an execution today."

The King's smile melted away. "What?"

"There isn't anyone left to be executed. You released everyone in the dungeon, remember? There isn't anyone left," Frederick said with obvious glee.

The King turned white, gripping the arms of his throne. He began to feel faint. "I need someone to hang," he whispered. He eyed Frederick.

King Cedric's head doctor entered the throne room. The King brightened.

"Good morning, Your Majesty. King Cedric sent me with the report on your advisor."

The King made a surreptitious hand gesture at Frederick. To the doctor, he said loudly, "Why, hello, Mr. Doctor! Yes, very good, I'm glad to hear you say so!"

The doctor eyed him dubiously. "Ahem. Your advisor has endured severe damage to Wernicke's area, a section of the brain that figures largely in linguistic function."

Behind him, Frederick snuck up, hefting his fiddle. The King strained to appear interested in what the doctor was saying.

"His resulting disorder, called Wernicke's Aphasia, causes patients to use nonsense words, often rendering their utterances incomprehensible."

Frederick hesitated, evidently reluctant to damage his prized instrument.

114

"Surprisingly, however, the patient excels at tests that gauge his comprehension and spatial abilities."

The King extracted a large bag of gold from his pocket. He held it up. Frederick smiled.

"The intelligence demonstrated by your advisor is far above average, leading me to wonder whether his mental proficiency might somehow have been enhanced by his accident, and whether—"

With a loud *crack*, Frederick's fiddle descended on the doctor's cranium, rendering him instantly unconscious. Staring at the ruined instrument, the fiddler began to sob loudly.

Larry entered into the throne room, and gaped from the doctor's inert form, to the weeping fiddler, to the King, who made a strangled sound.

Slowly, an ominous grin crept across the bespectacled linguist's face.

The King swallowed.

*

The throng teemed as the King made his way toward the gallows with Elizabeth on his arm.

"I had no idea so many people attend these things," said the King.

"Disgusting, isn't it?" said Elizabeth.

The King reserved comment.

Earl too drew near the gallows, pushing King Cedric's doctor in front of him. A black bag covered the prisoner's head.

The royal executioner remained utterly impassive. He was a hard man. He had once swallowed an egg raw, for the sole purpose of accosting fellows in bars and asking, "Have you ever swallowed an egg, *raw?*"

"That man looks vaguely familiar," said Elizabeth, studying the prisoner.

The King fidgeted nervously. King Cedric and his people were currently combing the castle for their head practitioner, unaware he was about to be hanged. The Linguists' Guild was working to make sure they didn't find out about the execution.

Larry had threatened to cure King Cedric of his ignorance, however, unless the King gave his guarantee the 'savages' would be executed. The linguist had caught wind of Elizabeth's protests, and wanted to ensure the Guild's theory of language was preserved.

In one hand the King held his Kingship (which would be forfeit, were King Cedric to learn of his deed), and in the other, his love for Elizabeth (who presently gazed up at him with large, hazel eyes). He envied the doctor.

Larry had arranged to give a Linguistics presentation before the hanging took place. He climbed the gallows, preceded by a man and woman dressed in rags and bound by chains.

"Ladies and Gentlemen!" the linguist bellowed, beaming toothily. "Since arriving in this

Kingdom, the Traveling Linguists' Guild has been bombarded with questions, such as 'What is Linguistics?', 'Who needs it anyhow?' and 'Who is that handsome man in the jester's hat?' Folks, I'm here to give you the answers: 'The study of language', 'You do', and 'Me, Larry'."

The crowd, unsure of how else to react, applauded wildly.

Larry's enthusiasm grew. "Linguistics is a relatively new discipline, and the easiest way to understand it is to see it in action. Allow me to introduce you all to John and Mary." He indicated the downtrodden figures beside him. "These willing participants travel everywhere with the Guild, teaching people just how the study of language works. Show 'em, Mary!"

"Save me from this hell," Mary moaned.

Larry beamed. "A linguist can tell you Mary's sentence contains only one clause, and, unlike regular English sentences, lacks a direct subject. John, have you anything to add?"

"Help," John said, apparently too weak to be polysyllabic.

"John's sentence consists of only a verb. English phrases generally possess a subject, verb and object—in that order—but it seems John and Mary are indulging us with some unique exceptions this fine afternoon!"

The crowd clapped.

With rare verboseness, Mary exclaimed, "They beat us every morning, and feed us colourless gruel!"

"An uncommon treat!" said Larry. "Mary's utterance contains a relative clause, and brilliantly illustrates English word order!"

Larry paused for more applause.

"You've been a great audience! Make sure to catch our acrobatic spectacle tomorrow evening!" Larry bounded from the gallows, dragging John and Mary along with him.

Next, the executioner prodded the doctor onto the stage and fitted the noose around his neck. Muffled screams could be heard from the black bag. The King felt Elizabeth's trembling hand envelope his own, and a thrill of excitement shot through him at the touch.

The trap was released, and for several minutes the doctor kicked madly. Earl looked coldly on.

Finally the doctor stopped twitching, and the crowd began to disperse. Earl began sawing at the rope holding up the body. "Don't kick like they used to, do they Mum?" the King heard a peasant boy say. His mother shushed him.

Elizabeth buried her head in the King's chest and wept. "Oh, Your Majesty, it's awful! It's terribly awful!"

"Awful doesn't begin to describe it," the King said as the last spectators wandered off. "I can't believe I've been letting folks attend these things for free!"

Elizabeth pulled back and shot him a stinging glare. She stalked away, leaving the King to wonder what she found so offensive about commerce.

*

He crept through his own castle, terrified of encountering King Cedric or his entourage. He had a nagging fear his nervousness would cause him to answer questions concerning the head doctor's whereabouts with "Purgatory!" or something in that vein.

A man shuffled toward him down the darkened hallway. The King couldn't make out his face, but he recognized the advisor's dragging gait. Quickly the monarch turned on his heel and headed in the opposite direction.

"Your Sidewaysness, wait! There is someplurb I have to tell you!"

The King walked faster.

"Sire! You must lishen! Your guests are plodding to assassishank you!"

The King whirled about and faced the monstrosity. "I can't understand you!" he cried, his voice wavering. A metal plate had been stitched over the advisor's fractured skull by King Cedric's doctors, and in the dark, it lent his silhouette a freakishly angular appearance.

"King Cedar is conspiring to have you murbled!" the abomination said.

The King grimaced. The man was spouting utter gibberish. What was it the head doctor had diagnosed him with? Vernon's Faucet?

"What business did you have, being resurrected?" the King said. "Every man gets one life, and yours ended, fair and square."

The advisor looked at the floor, as though the comment saddened him.

"And why are you haunting *me*, anyhow? I wasn't even the direct cause of your death—not that I didn't consider causing it, many times!"

The advisor's gaze suddenly shifted past the King. In the dark, the widening of his eyes was barely discernible. "Watch out, my leech! There's a quiver behind you!"

The King frowned. "Did you just call me a leech?"

As it turned out, there *was* a quiver behind the King. There was also an arrow, a bow and an archer.

The quiet *twang* of the taut bowstring was just barely preceded by the advisor tackling the King head-on. They both fell noisily to the marble.

Pattering footsteps receded down the hall. The advisor helped the King up.

"This is inconceivable!" the King growled, his ire fully roused. "I've told the staff countless times: no archery in the corridors!"

Even on the advisor's ruined face, incredulity at the King's stupidity proclaimed itself.

"Now, what were you saying?"

"They're troshing to keel you!" the advisor said.

"What?"

"They want you deadified!"

"Sorry?"

"Your life is in dagger!"

"Listen, I'm too busy for this. You're wasting even more of my time in death than you did while alive. Now, I have some serious avoiding to do. Excuse me." The King jogged away down the hall.

"King Cedric V is arranging to have you exterminated!" the advisor finally said, and smacked his metal plate in disbelief.

*

The King paused in the hall outside his throne room to catch his breath. He smiled, pleased with himself. He had traversed the halls without once encountering King Cedric or his staff.

He snuck into the throne room, and nearly suffered a stroke upon seeing who was assembled there.

To begin, King Cedric lounged in a throne the King had never seen before. It dwarfed his own in all respects: size, glamour, and, no doubt, cost.

"Do you like it, sire?" the visiting King asked him. Cold suspicion laced his tone. "I had it constructed since arriving. I can't abide regular chairs."

In the King's own throne sat the Wisest Man Alive and Eliza, snuggling in exactly the same way Eliza and the King used to.

And brooding in a corner, glowering at his former girlfriend and the Wisest Man Alive, was Frederick. He was clearly inebriated, and looked odd without a fiddle.

As if the aforementioned parties did not contribute sufficiently to the King's agitation, his mother stood between the thrones with hands on hips, overseeing the whole sordid enterprise.

His mother spearheaded the assault. "You look awful, boy. Don't you ever have your clothes pressed?"

The King fingered his attire abashedly.

She continued: "I guess you regret locking your mother in the dungeon now, don't you?" King Cedric raised his eyebrows. "No one to iron your wrinkly clothes for two years. I always knew you wouldn't amount to anything."

"But Mother," the King said. "I'm a King!"

"And a bloody terrible one, at that. Can't control the media without blowing it up, can't muster an army to defend yourself—can't even hold down a stable relationship!"

The Wisest Man Alive took up the torch. "On that note, I believe I've determined the source of your romantic issues, sire. In short, evolution has failed you. Males of our race are driven to flaunt their strengths in front of as many females as possible—that's how mating works. In your case, however, there are no strengths to exhibit. And so you flit from woman to woman, never able to establish anything worthwhile, because you lack a foundation on which to build."

The King growled. "That sounds like treason, to me."

"Actually," King Cedric said, "in the Northern Realm, we would call that 'freedom of speech'. You know: the uncensored expression of opinions and ideas. Don't you have anything like that in this Kingdom?"

"I don't like you much, either, Your Majesty," Frederick put in.

The King bristled. To think he should have to endure such a barrage in his own throne room! He already did most of his suffering in here; he certainly didn't need this added abuse.

"What are *you* doing here?" the King asked the Wisest Man Alive.

"I invited him," King Cedric V answered. "The Wisest Man Alive and I have been close correspondents for almost a decade, now. I don't get to see him nearly enough, and I was delighted to meet his fiancée."

"*Fiancée?*" Frederick snarled.

Eliza beamed. "That's right, Frederick. We're getting married." She kissed the Wisest Man Alive, and all present uncomfortably averted their gaze.

"I won't be attending the wedding," the King said.

"That's okay, Your Majesty," Eliza said. "You're not invited."

Presently, a servant the King didn't recognize entered the throne room with a tray bearing six sweating goblets.

"Ah, here is my manservant," King Cedric said, "with our drinks. It is only right the host should drink first. What would you like?" he asked the King.

Except for Frederick's, every gaze turned to the King. He also noticed the servant's arrival brought about a tense silence among those assembled. He frowned.

The servant gravitated toward the King. "What would you like, sire?" he asked. His eyes darted anxiously.

"Mead, if you have it," the King answered slowly.

The servant lifted the goblet situated in the very center of the tray. "That's this one. There you are, Your Majesty."

The King hesitated, and said, "On second thought, I'll have brandy."

King Cedric started perceptibly, and the Wisest Man Alive entered a coughing fit. The servant stammered, completely at a loss for what to do. "Um—er—I—"

Finally, the man realized he could do nothing but give the King another drink and continue around the room.

Keeping track of the goblet he'd refused, the King saw it ended up with the Wisest Man Alive. As everyone received their drinks, the conversation entered an awkward lull. The King continued to watch the old man. Finally, the Wisest Man Alive raised the suspicious goblet to his lips.

The King stopped holding his breath. He had been under the impression the goblet the servant seemed so keen to give him contained poison, but clearly that was daft. The paranoia that haunts rulers was strong with him today.

They finished drinking, and gradually the others began to depart the throne room. Cups were set down on the tray for the servant to collect later. Soon, only the King and Frederick remained.

The King approached the tray and studied the cups. He gasped, and steadied himself. One of the goblets was still full.

"Frederick," the King said, his voice trembling. "I think they're trying to kill me." He paused. "And I think my mother's helping them."

Frederick hiccupped. "Personally, I hope they succeed."

*

The King entered his private bathroom. "Good morning," he said as he passed the man bathing in the fountain-sized bath tub.

He stopped. He turned around. He returned to the man and lifted the damp towel that covered his face.

"King Cedric!"

The visiting monarch awoke with a start. Bubbles frothed over the sides and onto the floor. "Oh. Your Majesty. Hello."

"What are you doing in my private bathroom?"

King Cedric glanced at the bath water, and then back at the King. "Why, I'm taking a bath."

"Yes, I can see that, but the door is clearly marked—"

"It's marked *Kings*. And I happen to be one."

"You—" began the King. He cleared his throat. "Yes, I suppose you are."

King Cedric nodded. "It's a very nice bathroom, you know. What's that strange porcelain bowl over there?" He was pointing at the bidet.

The King ignored the question. "This is *my* bathroom!"

"Yes, and I am your guest."

"But—"

"Your Majesty, if you didn't wish others to use your bathroom, you should have indicated as much. As it stands, the door says *Kings*. Now, would you please pass the soap?"

The King glared for a few moments, his mouth working. He gave up, and stalked out.

"Close the door as you leave!" King Cedric called after him.

The King went in the bathroom marked *Lords*. It was cramped, and contained only a small toilet and wash basin.

He perched moodily, and was almost finished when he realized there was no toilet paper.

*

Larry accosted the King at an intersection of two hallways. From another direction, Elizabeth approached. Both looked pleased with his presence in particular, but dissatisfied with the King in general.

For two very different reasons.

Larry's tone was clipped. "You've yet to sign any orders concerning the barbarians' extermination, Your Highness. The only decree you uttered was to us alone, with no official witnesses present. If we discover you were only posturing, sire, you'll soon regret it. Linguistics is a *very* powerful discipline."

Elizabeth buzzed with rage. "Your Highness, if you execute an entire race, not only will your soul be damned, but I shan't love you anymore. And I *do* love you, sire. You are the best listener I've ever met."

The King grinned feebly at them. He addressed Larry's concerns first. "Larry," he said matter-of-factly. Thinking better of it, he

122

warmed his tone. "Larry! These things take time. You don't just execute an entire culture all at once. Imagine the paperwork! First you have to book appointments—my executioner has a lot on his plate. Then, you have to wash the noose after each hanging. Would you want to get hanged with a dirty noose?" Larry opened his mouth angrily. "Of course you wouldn't," the King said. "And after all those executions, it's time to commission death certificates. For every single hanging!" The King smiled. "Perhaps you can see my dilemma."

He turned to Elizabeth. "Elizabeth!" She growled. "*Liz*. Of course I'm not going to execute an *entire race*! That would be madness! It's just that in a moment of weakness, I made a promise I couldn't keep. I didn't even realize I couldn't keep it at the time. But I do now, and so I plan to stall the supplicants in question with acts of pointless bureaucracy, in hopes that they'll go away, or that they can be quietly done away with at some point in the future."

Both linguists stared at him in consternation.

"Which of those declamations did you actually mean?" they asked in unison.

The King looked from linguist to linguist. He sensed he'd messed up somehow.

"Neither of them!"

Larry spat: "Worthless bureaucrat!"

Elizabeth hissed: "Lying pig!"

The King gestured broadly, encompassing all three of them. "Conflict of interest!"

Larry rounded on Elizabeth. "You're jeopardizing our unified theory."

"You've taken leave of your senses!"

"You don't know what it is to be a linguist!"

"You've forsaken morality!" She plucked at his jester's hat. "And fashion sense."

They glared at each other, oblivious to all else. The King silently backed away. Once he reached a safe distance, he turned and fled.

*

The King cowered behind a statue, darting glances up and down the hallway. In the past week, he had nearly been assassinated in the

123

throne room, in the dining chamber, in the hallways and in his private restroom. As well, the advisor turned up in bed with him three times.

He snuck around the statue and began to creep down the hall.

Larry and Elizabeth pestered him constantly, King Cedric never stopped criticizing him, and his mother eyed him accusingly in the corridors. If one more person found fault with him, the King was certain he would snap.

"Your Majesty, I've come to have a talk with you."

The King spun around. He rubbed his eyes. The girl standing in front of him couldn't possibly be the girl standing in front of him.

It was Alice.

"What's this I hear about you being in love?"

The King blinked. "What?"

"You heard me. I know what you've been doing. I know you're seeing another woman."

The King finally mustered a reply. "So?"

"You said you loved me! I was 'the rose whose splendour a name does no justice'." She glared. "You're a fake."

"But that was a year ago!"

"Is your love so short-lived?"

"You rejected me! You spurned me in the worst possible way!"

"Maybe I was playing hard to get."

"You told me to go ahead and cut my own heart out!"

Alice shook her head. "I've had enough of your games. I didn't come to talk. I came to give you this." And she slapped the King with all her might.

The King's ears rang as Alice stalked off.

"Women!" he said with emphasis.

He retired to his bedchambers, massaging his throbbing cheek. He hid under the covers, but knew better than to feel safe.

He wanted to cry. "I'm surrounded by enemies. I've just been slapped. I'm being haunted by my zombie advisor." He paused. "And I think he's coming on to me."

"I'm not coming on to you," the advisor protested from beside him. "I'm trying to wargle you."

The King leaped from the bed, shrieking. "*Wargle* me?" he said. "*What in the gods' names is that?*"

He ran from the bed chambers in his pyjamas.

"Warn!" the advisor corrected himself angrily, having once again rediscovered the ability to speak the instant the King left. "Warn, warn, warn, warn, *warn!*"

The King ran to the throne room, curling up in his throne and whimpering. Nearby, King Cedric's throne towered over him. Finally his breathing slowed, and he slept.

In his dream he was still in the throne room, with daylight streaming in. He looked around—everything was as it should be. There wasn't anything strange going on at all.

He woke up screaming.

*

The King still sat in his throne wearing his pyjamas when King Cedric entered the following morning, accompanied by one of his staff.

"Good morning," the visiting monarch greeted him. "This is my throne polisher. Your throne looks like it could use a good burnish."

The throne polisher promptly stepped forward. Suddenly, a machete fell from a fold in his robes with a loud clatter. He jerked, picking it up with haste. He looked at the King. The blade gleamed wickedly. He stepped forward.

The gods chose that moment to smile upon the King, and Frederick walked into the throne room. "Why does that man have a machete?" he asked casually.

The King, making a mental note to ensure the fiddler received this week's pay cheque, repeated the question: "I'm curious about that as well. Why *does* he have a machete, King Cedric?"

His guest grinned disarmingly. "Your Majesty, it isn't what it seems. My employee is merely an aspiring sword-swallower, who wishes to one day join the Traveling Linguists' Guild. He began with toothpicks, graduated to butter knives, and has finally worked his way up to machetes."

Both King Cedric and his employee adopted smug expressions, evidently pleased with their sleek evasion.

"Inspiring," the King said dryly. "Can we have a demonstration?"

They both turned white. The alleged machete-swallower began to stammer.

"Of course you can!" King Cedric said weakly. "Go on," he urged his staff member.

The throne polisher, trembling, tilted his head back and began to insert the blade into his mouth. He'd managed to swallow about an eighth without serious injury when he glanced at his employer fearfully. King Cedric gestured anxiously for him to continue.

Somehow, the entire machete disappeared—hilt and all. The throne polisher appeared more surprised than his audience. He gave a sickly smile.

"Good show," King Cedric said in a strained voice. "You may go, now."

His employee exited, careful to maintain a perfectly vertical posture. When the throne room's door closed, a hideous shriek could be heard from the hallway.

"He gets really excited when he does that," King Cedric said.

*

Frederick heard someone coming, and hid behind a giant vase in one of the hallway's alcoves. From his hiding place he spied the Wisest Man Alive and Eliza.

The pair stopped when they reached the alcove. The fiddler tensed.

"Isn't it great to be young and in love?" Eliza said, gazing up at him wistfully.

"Well, it's great to be in love," said the Wisest Man Alive, "but I've rather forgotten what it's like to be young!"

They laughed as though it were the funniest joke in the world, and continued down the hall.

Behind the vase Frederick scowled, and began rocking back and forth. He tapped his fingers together with insane malevolence. He dwelled obsessively on death, and the myriad ways it might be visited upon the old man who'd stolen his girlfriend.

*

Other than the King, the throne room was empty. He looked out the windows, but instead of his Kingdom, he saw only blinding white

126

light. As well, the throne room lacked a door. The one normally there had vanished.

The King thought he could hear a voice—a voice that sounded intimately familiar—but was unable to make out what it said, or from whence it came. It murmured constantly in the background.

A bucket of purple paint sat near the wall opposite his throne. He approached it and, having nothing else to do, he withdrew the brush it contained and made a stroke on the wall.

With a greedy slurping sound, the paint disappeared. The King frowned, and placed his hand on the wall where it had been. Completely dry. The wall had absorbed it.

The King made more strokes, which, like the first, quickly vanished. Chuckling, he drew a smiling face. It seemed strangely melancholy as it too was absorbed.

He tried some paint on his hand, but nothing happened. Contented, he studied his newly purple index finger. The colour suited him.

Suddenly, the paint covering his finger turned pitch black. He yelped. Something flickered in his peripheral vision, and he swung his head around. Part of the wall had begun to melt. It simply dripped away, revealing a growing patch of white light.

Similar patches appeared in other places—the floor, the walls, the ceiling. The entire throne room was dissolving. And with this revelation, a perfect calm descended upon the King.

He woke up in his king-sized bed, sweating profusely.

*

The King's fist hovered uncertainly, poised to knock. He dropped it to his side again. He couldn't decide which he would prefer: getting assassinated or speaking with his mother more than absolutely necessary.

Finally he did knock, which provoked a good deal of shuffling about on the other side of the wooden door. The door opened a few inches, revealing his mother in a hastily donned dressing gown. "What?" she barked.

"I need to speak with you."

His mother glanced over her shoulder, and turned back. "You can't come in."

"This is *my* castle!" the King said, and pushed past her.

He stopped, his mouth open. A shirtless man was standing near the bed, fastening his pants. It was his former stable master. The King made a strangled sound.

"Guards!" he yelled.

"Shut up!" said his mother.

A pair of armed men rushed into the chamber. They were King Cedric's.

"What's the matter?" they asked.

"Throw this man in the dungeon!"

"Sorry, sire, we can't do that."

The King gaped. "Why in blazes not?"

"Because King Cedric has ordered that no one is to be thrown in the dungeon anymore."

"What say does King Cedric have in anything?"

The guards were firm. "We apologize, Your Highness." They left the chamber.

The former stable master shrugged. "Guess I'll be heading off, then." He winked at the King. "Nice seeing you again, Your Majesty." He finished putting on his shirt, and left.

The King began to scream, and stomp around the room. He tried punching things, but soon stopped when his fist started to hurt.

He finally calmed down, and his mother raised an eyebrow. "What's wrong, son? Not allowed to lock people away anymore? What a pity."

The King scowled. He was still breathing heavily. "Never mind that. I've come about the conspiracy."

Her eyes widened innocently. "Conspiracy? What conspiracy?"

"The conspiracy to kill me. Of which you're a conspirator."

She looked at the carpet. "Oh. That conspiracy."

"Yes, *that* one. I was just wondering why you'd want to murder your only son."

His mother looked at him in surprise. "I think the appropriate question is why *wouldn't* I want to murder my only son." She paused. "Oh, and while we're on the topic: you aren't my only son."

The King decided it best to ignore this last revelation.

128

His mother continued. "You're a cad, and a disgrace to the family name. You've given me nothing but grief." She eyed his attire. "And you refuse to iron your clothes."

"I'll start ironing my clothes! Just call off the conspiracy!"

"And all that *education*." She shuddered at the word. "I told you it was a big waste of money. Good boys help their mother run the family business. You might have taken it over."

"But you sold *shoehorns!*"

His mother glared. "Very well-made shoehorns, yes. I was the most respected shoehorn vendor for miles. Anyway. I'm having you murdered, and that's that. Get out of my chambers." She pointed imperiously at the door.

The King pouted, and walked sulkily toward the exit, kicking his heels.

"Oh, and if you see him, tell your old stable master he can drop by again tomorrow night."

*

"Your Majesty!" Larry hailed him loudly. "Stay right there!"

The King grimaced. "Be quiet, linguist! I'm trying to evade assassination."

Larry's countenance became grave. "Who's trying to assassinate you?"

"No one," the King said, immediately realizing his mistake.

"King Cedric is trying to kill you?"

"Of course not! Don't be absurd."

The linguist's brow furrowed. "But if you die, the Guild's unified theory will as well. We'll never be able to find someone as morally destitute as you are." He sighed. "King Cedric must be dealt with."

The King seized the linguist's lapels. "Stay—away—from—King—Cedric! If he discovers my knowledge of the conspiracy, I'm as good as dead!"

"Aren't you as good as dead if we *don't* kill him?"

"I seriously doubt your ability to kill King Cedric."

"Again, sire, you underestimate the Guild." The linguist strode purposefully down a connecting corridor. "By sunset, the traitorous monarch will have met his makers," he called over his shoulder.

The King slumped against a nearby wall, and despaired.

*

At sunset the King stood in the Royal Square, standing in front of a stockade that contained Larry. He slapped him.

"You imbecile!"

Larry rolled his eyeballs to look up at the King. He smiled. "Not to worry, Your Highness. The Guild is on high alert. My imprisonment is a trifling matter—it doesn't mean a thing, where your safety is concerned."

Earlier that evening, Larry snuck into King Cedric's chambers with a poison-tipped dagger. The monarch's guards apprehended the linguist within roughly seven seconds.

"You're right about that," the King said. "I'm still as near death as I was before!"

His fiddler crossed the Square, approaching the stockade dejectedly.

"Good evening, Frederick," the King said half-heartedly when the fiddler drew near.

Frederick's eyes were filled with remorse. This was especially noteworthy, since for Frederick to look at the King with anything other than murderous intent was rare.

"There's something I need to get off my chest," the fiddler rasped, as if on the verge of tears. "I—I killed."

The King cleared his throat. "You killed? That sentence requires an object to be of any use to me. Who did you kill?"

"I killed a man."

"Okay. That eliminates half the population. "Which one?"

Frederick turned away. He swallowed. He fidgeted. Finally, he turned back to face the King.

"The Wisest—"

The King flinched, praying Frederick was about to say "donkey."

"—Man—"

The King's shoulders slumped.

"—Alive. Except, he isn't anymore. Alive, that is."

"You've ruined me." The King leaned heavily on the stockade.

Frederick failed to make eye contact. "Yes. I have. They already declared you deposed at the castle. They're publicly announcing that you ordered me to kill the Wisest Man Alive. A warrant has been issued for both our deaths."

Larry twisted in his stockade with futility. "Those vermin! The Guild will never allow it!"

"Actually," Frederick said, "the Guild members attacked King Cedric's staff after the warrant was signed, but were quickly repelled from the castle." Frederick coughed. "A warrant has been issued for their deaths, too."

The linguist finally lost his irksome certainty, and began to sweat.

"Why, Frederick?" said the King. "Why did you bring this upon me?"

"I couldn't help it! I was lingering about the castle drawbridge when that vile old man passed by with his dawdling, decrepit gait. He's been provoking me ever since he arrived at the castle—always kissing and snuggling with Eliza in plain view of everyone! There was a weapon near the drawbridge, and there was no one else present, and so I just sort of—killed him."

"What was the weapon?"

"A garden spade."

"A garden spade?"

"Yes."

"And that made you think of killing?"

"Um…yes."

"Funny, that. I usually think of gardens when I see garden spades."

Frederick paused. "No, it really isn't funny at all."

"How did they know you did it?"

"Well, as soon as I was finished one of Cedric's servants happened along and screamed, 'It's the fiddler and he's killed the Wisest Man Alive!' That blew my cover somewhat. I ran. I met a Guild member fleeing the castle, and he told me what happened."

A trumpet sounded in the distance, and then another, close by.

"Your Majesty," Frederick whispered. "They're hunting you! They're hunting *us!*"

"We must escape," the King said, his eyes wide.

"We can't. They've blocked all the main roads."

The King's thoughts whirled. "What about the cart path that leads to Mount High? Have they blocked that?"

The fiddler looked at him incredulously. "I doubt it. Why would they expect us to flee to the house whose occupant we murdered? It would be insane!"

The King grinned. "Exactly."

Understanding dawned on Frederick. "Your Majesty, that's...that's brilliant. I'm shocked."

"Commend me later," the King said. "Lavishly. But right now, we survive. Let's go."

Presently, a bearded man dressed in rags approached them. "Excuse me?" he said. "Are you the King?"

"Yes," the King said. "And I'm very busy."

The ragged man cleared his throat, regarding him sternly. "I'm the prophet, Pablo. I come bearing a grim prophecy."

The King grimaced. "Will it take long?"

The prophet ignored the question, continuing in ominous tones. "Sire, your hubris has blinded you. You think yourself invincible, but your downfall looms. You will lose the throne, and you will have your lot thrown in with one who loathes you."

Frederick and the King shared a look.

"What?" Pablo said.

"I just lost my throne," said the King. "And now I'm escaping with Frederick. Who hates me."

"I really do," Frederick said.

The prophet fingered his ear. "So it's already happened, then?"

"Yes."

"The prophecy's been fulfilled?"

"Well, no," said the King. "For a prophecy to be fulfilled, it has to precede the events prophesied."

"In other words—"

"You're a hack."

"Untrue!" Pablo protested. "Wholly untrue. I've accurately prophesied lots of stuff. Remember the drought two summers back? I predicted that!"

The King remained sceptical.

"And the siege! Oh, ho, ho, did I ever predict the siege!"

132

"Well I wish you'd done it in my presence!" the King said. "I would have stocked up on toilet paper."

"I'm an accomplished prophet!" Pablo insisted. "My timing is off lately, that's all."

"Prove it, then," said Frederick. "Forecast something useful."

"Hmm," said the prophet. "Ahh—this is such short notice…"

"He's useless," said Frederick. "Let's go."

"Wait! Your Majesty," Pablo began, and again adopted his most portentous prophesying voice. "You will lead a very long life!"

The King scoffed. "That's a sham. If I do live a long time, you'll be right, and if I don't, I won't be around to call you on it!"

The two fugitives started across the Square.

"You will make a surprising discovery!" Pablo shouted after them, but the King and Frederick weren't listening. The prophet slumped dejectedly.

"Hey! Guys!" It was Larry.

They turned back. Fear twisted the linguist's features.

"You're not going to leave me here, are you? What with the death warrant, and all? That would be pretty inconsiderate, wouldn't it?"

The King and Frederick turned once more and exited the Royal Square.

*

Like clumsy, noisy shadows they moved through the town, sticking mostly to the alleys between houses. Trumpets blared all around them. Mobs of raging peasants, who had long been waiting for an excuse to string up their King, charged up and down the roadways, their torches dancing merrily.

"You may not be very popular," Frederick said, "but I'll give you this: you sure know how to draw attention."

They both ducked as a group of peasants charged by.

Before King Cedric arrived, the King had never truly felt fear before. When the Kingdom Crier had desecrated his public image, he had been irritated. During the siege, he was uncomfortable. While watching Sir Forsythe and Duke Edward fight to the death, he'd experienced an exaggerated trepidation. Everything had seemed a game to him. Tonight, however, he looked mortality in its pitiless eyes, just like every man he'd ever sent to the guillotine.

Finally, they reached the cart path. They stopped. At its mouth, a feminine silhouette awaited them.

Elizabeth stepped out of the shadows. "Your Majesty," she said breathlessly.

The former King hesitated, and then shook his head sadly. "No. Not anymore."

"I know. We tried to stop them. The Guild fought in your name—if not for reasons that are exactly respectable. King Cedric's men are numerous, however, and we failed." She paused. "Plus, linguists aren't the brawniest of folk."

The King nodded, quite able to relate. "How did you know to come here?"

"I anticipated your psychology. I figured you were the kind of man whose lunacy would prove an advantage at times like this."

"Aha!" Frederick said. "Lunacy, that's it! Not brilliance at all."

The King scowled.

"Sire," Elizabeth said, "I've come to ask—nay, beg—that you take me with you. These past few days I have discovered deep feelings for you. I pray if you look in your heart, you will find something that resonates with mine."

For a long while, the King remained silent. It occurred to him that Elizabeth was the perfect woman for him. She was intelligent, beautiful, and apparently able to live with his moral poverty after all. Perhaps a little chatty, but unlike Alice or Eliza, she loved him, and seemed devoted to him alone.

"No," he said. "I've lost interest." He turned to his fiddler. "Come on, Frederick." He brushed past her and started alomg the cart path.

Frederick remained where he was. "Are you insane?" he called after the King. "You have a stunning young maiden throwing herself at you!"

"Will you hurry up?" the King shouted over his shoulder. "We'll never climb Mount High at this rate."

The fiddler shrugged, apologized to Elizabeth, and hurried after him.

"Be safe!" the linguist called after him, her voice wavering. "I love you!"

"Talks a lot, doesn't she?" said the King.

*

Together they struggled up Mount High. The climb seemed even more treacherous than the King recalled. He supposed the darkness had something to do with it.

"Why is it called Mount High?" Frederick asked.

"I hope you're joking."

They climbed on. From time to time, the King glanced back at the city. Torches still bobbed along the streets, but at a less fevered pace. None of them approached Mount High.

"So," the King said at length, panting. "Who do you think is the Wisest Man Alive now the Wisest Man Alive is dead?"

"Not sure," the fiddler said. "Sir Forsythe is pretty wily. Maybe it's him."

The King sneered. "Are you serious? I think you're missing what's right in front of you."

"Sire, I can assure you: you aren't the Wisest Man Alive."

The King harrumphed. "How can you be so sure?"

"Well, for one, if you were the least bit wise you'd still have your throne."

"And if the Wisest Man Alive had been wise, he'd still be alive! If you ask me, the title's legitimacy is in question!"

Frederick shook his head. They carried on in silence.

Inwardly, the King speculated about who might get the throne, now that he no longer occupied it. He wondered if King Cedric was capable of managing two Kingdoms at once. He wondered if his mother would pester Cedric as much as she pestered the King.

Finally, the King and Frederick attained the summit. The hut situated in the middle of the plateau was just as ramshackle as the King remembered.

Frederick stared. "*That's* where the Wisest Man Alive lives?"

"Lived," the King said. "And yes. I suppose being wise makes you something of an ascetic."

Frederick approached the wooden door, placing his hands on its splintered planks. "And this is where he asked his riddles?"

The King nodded.

"What did he ask you?"

"Erm, something about the town garbage wagon. I didn't answer it, though."

"And he let you in anyway?"

The King nodded. He ran his hand over the gouge he had made with the axe.

Without further ado, they entered. The King took more time to look around than he had during his previous visit. After all, this hovel was their home for the indefinite future.

The rickety table still sat in the center of the room, with all the dirt swept underneath it. Bookshelves and cupboards lined the room's perimeter, and a modest cot sat in the corner. The King made a mental note to ensure he claimed it first.

"But where did he relieve himself?" Frederick asked, a little sheepish.

The King shifted uneasily. "The Wisest Man Alive didn't place much of a premium on hygiene."

The explanation didn't dampen Frederick's enthusiasm. He flitted about the room, poking at nooks and crannies. Several gadgets caught his attention for long moments, and he skimmed some of the Wisest Man Alive's many dissertations.

After his initial look about, the King plopped in one of the table's two chairs.

"How do you think he passed the time up here?" Frederick said.

"Who knows? Let's find something to eat." The King rose again, and began rummaging through the cupboards.

Frederick picked up a hefty, unbound manuscript. "Hey, what's this?" he said, and flipped through a few pages. "Good gods!"

The King glanced at the fiddler indifferently. "What is it?"

The fiddler shook his head, sitting down at the table with the manuscript. "I don't know. But—well, listen to how it starts: 'The glass chimes on the front door tinkled and the Kingdom's sole glassblower raised his head. "Now who?" he said, and peeped out from his cramped back room, only to hastily withdraw his head.'" He turned to the next page. "I think it's a story."

The passage made something stir in the King's memory. He leaned across the table, trying to read the text upside down. "What's it about?"

"I think—" Frederick began, and then stopped. He looked at the King. "I think it's about you."

"About *me?*" The King squealed with delight. "Give it here!"

Frederick handed him a chunk of text. The King opened to a random page.

"'The King wasn't above ordering a man killed on a whim,'" he read aloud. "That's ludicrous! I never hang anyone without thinking about it first. Well, not very often. This narrative is biased."

Frederick wasn't listening. His face had grown stony, and now he looked at the King with flashing eyes. He held a page in front of the King, indicating a particular paragraph.

Slowly, the King read the passage: "'Eliza lounged in the King's lap, who in turn lounged on the throne. She kissed him passionately.'" The King's throat constricted. "Entirely untrue!" he managed. "What a heretical, fictitious story the Wisest Man Alive was writing!"

"Indeed," Frederick said. "I was right to murder the lying swine." He stood up and approached the door. "I'll just be throwing this to the four winds."

"Wait!" the King cried. "That's my biography! Unhand that manuscript!"

Frederick whirled about, his face a frightening contortion. "I thought you said it was false," he hissed.

The King swallowed. "Of course it's false! All biographers embellish the lives of their subjects—else they wouldn't be worth writing about!"

For a long moment, Frederick glared at the King. Finally he stalked to the table and tossed the papers onto it. The King quickly gathered them up, clutching them tenderly to his chest.

He looked at the last page. "It ends after the arrival of the Traveling Linguists' Guild. That must be when King Cedric invited the Wisest Man Alive to my castle, and he had to stop writing."

"King Cedric's castle," Frederick said.

The King ignored this. "It's too bad the Wisest Man Alive had to die," he said. "Now he'll never finish it."

*

Eliza walked through the market, feeling smothered in her black mourning robes. It had been a week since the former King and his fiddler escaped. They had yet to be found.

"I'm sorry for your loss, ma'am. Your fiancé was a fine man."

She nodded, graciously accepting the pauper's condolences. Much of the populace had approached her to offer sympathy. Eliza had become quite an icon throughout the town, ever since the simultaneous exodus of her two previous lovers. There were whispers that perhaps what the Kingdom really needed was a queen.

Most of the Traveling Linguists' Guild had managed to escape into the wilderness, with a few notable exceptions. Larry, found still locked in the stockades, had been promptly executed. Before dying he tried to barter the past King's whereabouts in return for the extermination of some tribe of natives, but no one listened to his wild ranting. Elizabeth, a linguist who specialized in communication among honeybees, had also been apprehended, but not killed. She was being detained as leverage in case the former King ever returned, despite her claims that he cared not a speck for her. It was just the kind of desperate thing you expected a prisoner to say.

The former King's mother had left the castle shortly after ensuring her son was properly usurped.

Eliza crossed the drawbridge, the guards bowing as she passed. She smiled. Perhaps being sovereign *would* be nice, but she would never accept the appointment.

King Cedric V portrayed the Northern Realm as a fair, democratic land, however since the former King's departure he had become quite a tyrant. He grew increasingly fond of hangings, and had made excellent friends with the royal executioner, Earl. The executioner's patterns of loyalty were affected exclusively by executions, and who was capable of commissioning them. Earl was more than happy to sate King Cedric's growing appetite.

Two days prior, King Cedric had been screaming about the lack of horses. "That bloody imbecile of a ruler sold all his mounts! All that remained in the stables when we checked was a mangy goat, who, when we opened its stall, skewered one of my men and took off!" King Cedric seethed. "Someone is going to get hanged for this."

Eliza was relieved King Cedric wouldn't be the one to inherit the throne.

She entered her rooms, where the Kingdom's next ruler sat at the writing desk, scribbling furiously. Unannounced, she snaked her arms about his neck from behind. He started, but after realizing who she was he greeted her warmly.

"Hello, Alice. I'm just finishing up this section. I'd like to finish the entire manuscript before I have to begin my duties."

Eliza stroked his beard. "How's the writing going?"

"A little forced at times, but relatively well for the most part. My subject's essence is a tedious one to capture." He paused. "It's a real bother, too, not having the rest of the manuscript in front of me. I must send someone to Mount High to fetch it."

"Good idea." Her beloved cared so much for his work. "How is the decoy doing?"

"He's recovering. The fiddler bludgeoned him quite thoroughly, but he's a strapping young fellow. Only seventy-six, you know. He'll make it."

Eliza giggled. "Frederick walked right into our trap. I knew he would."

"We made him very angry during the past couple of weeks. I often feared he would act too early."

She continued to run her fingers through his flowing facial hair. "None of that, now. The important thing is he *didn't* act too early. And as soon as things settle down, the Kingdom will receive its rightful ruler—you."

Smiling gratefully, he stood up and swept her into his arms. They shared a drawn-out kiss.

When they finally parted, Eliza smiled back up at him. She wondered how many women could truthfully claim to have locked lips with the Wisest Man Alive.

K ♣

The King
of
Clubs

♣
K

"What should I call you, now?" Frederick asked the King. "I mean, 'Your Highness' doesn't really fit anymore. You've been dethroned."

The King considered this. "I suppose you can carry on as normal. By now I've grown used to 'sire' and 'my liege'. Besides, I fully intend to reclaim my throne."

"No, I don't think it's appropriate any longer. I think you need a new name." Frederick smiled. "From now on, I'm going to call you Mud."

Mud sighed, and replaced his head on the rickety tabletop. He was tired of waking every other day with an aching back. He was tired of being hungry, and he was tired of never shaving. The Wisest Man Alive had been abstemious in every sense of the word, and the gluttonous former King reviled him for it.

"You know, I'm surprised he even owned a shack. I think it was a particularly selfish move on his part. Altruistic, my left armpit."

On the table lay the manuscript he had pored over innumerable times. It contained the story of Mud's life, and his dejection grew with each reading. Even more depressing, it was completely accurate. Despite what he'd told Frederick to placate him.

Mud didn't know how the Wisest Man Alive had, from a remote mountaintop, inferred every last detail of Mud's life for the past year and a half. Even the conversations in the manuscript were, as far as he could remember, verbatim. He supposed being the Wisest Man Alive had to count for something.

Mud stood up, wincing. He and Frederick took turns using the single cot, but it was only slightly better than the floor. The nearest mattress was miles away. Even blankets were nowhere to be found. A single scrap of clothing would have sufficed, or at least helped, but apparently the Wisest Man Alive had limited himself to just the one outfit.

He stepped outside. The sun was rising in the east, bringing a glorious morning to the Kingdom. Somehow, he appreciated the view more now that he no longer owned it.

He cast his gaze about, taking it all in. The castle, inexplicably situated at the bottom of a valley. The royal polo pitch, unused now that Mud had been overthrown. The pile of rubble, where the offices of the accursed Kingdom Crier once stood.

The fiddler joined him, clutching his back and hobbling. He glared at the former monarch, out of habit. Mud wasn't sure why they hadn't murdered each other yet. He had certainly considered offing Frederick, if only because he was hungry. It reminded him of the siege, and the cannibalistic notions he had entertained then as well.

"Have you noticed it hasn't rained since you were dethroned?" Frederick said.

Mud grimaced. "I don't want to talk about it."

Movement on the slopes of Mount High attracted Mud's attention. He frowned. "Someone is climbing up."

Frederick squinted, and fright tightened his features. "We have to hide."

They ran around to the rear of the hut.

At length they heard someone scramble onto the plateau, scattering loose pebbles. The shack's door opened with an audible squeak, and slammed. Hesitantly, they peered through the grimy window situated in the back of the hovel.

Apparently housecleaning had been beneath the Wisest Man Alive, as well—through the grime, they were unable to discern the visitor's identity. The silhouette of a man approached the table, where Mud's unfinished biography sat. He picked it up and turned to leave.

"He's taking the manuscript!" said Mud.

Frederick seized him before he could run to the front. "Come off it!" the fiddler whispered. "You'll blow our cover!"

Mud wrenched himself from the musician's grasp and scampered around to intercept the intruder. Snatching a hefty chunk of wood from a pile near the door, he clobbered the man with it as he emerged. The intruder crumpled.

Frederick joined him, and gasped. "You halfwit! Now we can't hide here any longer!"

Mud stopped to think about this. "Why not?"

"Because if we keep him here, they'll notice his absence and come looking. But if we let him go, he'll tell them we're here and they'll still come looking!"

"Oh," Mud said. It didn't seem like such an unfortunate thing to him.

"Who is he, anyhow?" They bent down to study the newcomer's face. "Good gods!"

It was the throne polisher—the aspiring sword swallower.

"I never thought I'd see this man again," said Mud. "I wonder how he removed the machete from his throat."

"It doesn't matter. Take his clothes off."

Mud eyed his companion. "Um, why?"

"Two reasons. First, they're probably a lot cleaner than ours, and second, he won't be able to make it down the mountain without them."

"Fair enough." Mud gathered the loose pages of the manuscript from where they'd fallen, and they set about stripping the throne polisher of his attire.

"Now we have three outfits," Frederick said. "He's about the same size as you and I, so we can take turns wearing the clean one."

The throne polisher woke up, noted his nakedness, and screamed. "What are you doing to me?"

"We're stranding you on this mountaintop," said Frederick.

"Oh. That's a relief. I thought you were going to…." He swallowed. "…never mind."

"Are the main roads still being guarded?" said Mud.

The throne polisher shook his head. "Now you've been properly usurped, they don't see you as much of a threat. In fact, they're hoping you've already left the Kingdom."

"What about the fiddler?" said Frederick. "Are they ready to let bygones be bygones? Can I go back to the castle?"

"Nope. They're still going to have you hanged on sight."

"Oh." Frederick shifted uncomfortably. "Well then. Guess I'm with you, old buddy." He patted Mud's shoulder gingerly.

Mud frowned.

Frederick took some dissertations written by the Wisest Man Alive for light reading, and they departed, leaving the naked throne polisher staring after them. The trek down Mount High was less strenuous than the climb up, but more treacherous. Several times Mud nearly found himself careening to his doom, or at least serious injury. He caught himself every time, though, and every time the fiddler looked disappointed.

When they finally reached the town they found the streets empty, except for a few stragglers heading in the direction of the castle. Frederick and Mud hid their faces under their hoods and approached one of them.

"Excuse me," Frederick said, masking his voice by way of making it ridiculously high-pitched. "Where is everybody?"

The peasant raised his eyebrows. "You haven't heard, ma'am? There's a parade about to begin. It's been the talk of the Kingdom for days."

"A parade?" Mud said. "Why didn't I get any parades?"

The peasant's brows furrowed thoughtfully. "Well, you've got to be pretty important. In any case, you can come watch this one. Follow me!"

The three of them continued toward the castle, eventually encountering a large throng lining the street.

"This is the parade route," their new friend said. He added in a whisper: "They say the new King will be at the very end."

Mud and Frederick exchanged glances.

A fanfare of trumpets sounded, and their attention was drawn down the street, where the parade had begun in earnest. The first to pass by was a marching band.

"Who's that fiddler?" Frederick shouted, forgetting to mask his voice. He clenched his fists. "He's completely out of time with the rest of the band! Go back to the banjo, you hack!"

Mud clamped a hand over Frederick's mouth. The peasant shot Frederick a strange look. "I could have sworn you were a woman."

Next in line were King Cedric V and his entourage. At the monarch's right hand was Mud's former executioner, and at his left, a stunning black-haired maiden.

"That's his royal concubine," the peasant said. "One of them, anyway."

"Why didn't you have any of those?" Frederick asked Mud. "Maybe then you might have kept your hands off of Alice."

The peasant's expression grew increasingly bemused.

A gang of downtrodden men passed next, dressed in drab clothing and bound by chains.

"Who are they?" Mud asked the peasant.

"Prisoners. King Cedric intends to have them hanged when the parade is over, in celebration of the new King's coronation."

Frederick's eyebrows climbed into his hair. "He's even more industrious than you were, Mud."

A second fanfare erupted, this one far more climactic than the first. The peasant began to tremble. "He's coming," he whispered, unable to contain his excitement.

A sumptuous sedan chair approached, carried by four burly men. Its velvet curtains were drawn. The men stopped directly in front of where Mud and Frederick stood. They put the sedan chair down and drew the curtains back.

As one, the crowd lining the street fell to its knees. Except for Mud and Frederick. They remained standing, and gaped in perfect astonishment.

The peasant pulled them down by their robes. They hit the ground with an unceremonious *thump*.

Mud turned to Frederick. "I thought you murdered him!"

"I did! I smashed him in the head with a garden spade!"

"I don't see any dents!"

One of the four chair-carriers stepped forward, raising his voice above the crowd's reverent murmur. "All hail the Wisest King Alive!"

The crowd cheered wildly. Luckily, Mud's heckling was drowned out.

When the carriage passed on, the peasant stood up and tugged once more on their robes. "Come on! Aren't you coming to the Royal Square? The new King is giving his first address!"

Reluctantly, they let themselves be dragged along. They reached the Square, where the Wisest Man—er, King—Alive had already taken the podium.

"What's that thing on his head?" Mud asked Frederick.

"A crown," came the incredulous reply.

"What's a crown?"

The crowd fell silent, and Frederick was unable to answer. The new King started his speech.

"Many of you have expressed concerns about my apparent reincarnation," the Wisest King Alive began, "and whether it was performed within the bounds of ethics. Well, I come to soothe your unease. I wasn't reincarnated, because I never really died. Come on up, Derm."

A man bearing a striking resemblance to the new King stepped onto the stage, and the Wisest King Alive threw an arm around his shoulder. The look-alike wore a bandage wrapped around his head. He smiled broadly at the crowd and waved.

"This young man is a decoy," the Wisest King Alive said. "He was bludgeoned with a garden spade last month near the castle drawbridge—but not bludgeoned to death. It is all part of an elaborate plot, you see, to usurp my predecessor: the ruthless tyrant."

No one in the crowd really understood this explanation. They all agreed the last King had been a jerk, though, so they applauded loudly.

The decoy left the stage. The new King continued: "If you're wondering what I intend to do with my newfound authority, the answer is simple. I intend to do everything the previous ruler didn't."

He paused. The crowd took a moment to mull this over, and then cheered their wildest cheer yet.

Mud felt his nails biting into his palms.

"I will tend to the sick," the Wisest King Alive said. "I will feed the poor. I will practise fair judgment." He eyed King Cedric. "Release the prisoners, Cedric."

The visiting monarch opened his mouth to protest. The new King silenced him with a level gaze.

Stony-faced, King Cedric declared his captives free to go. They rushed from the Royal Square before the new King could change his mind. Apparently they'd forgotten King Cedric held the only keys to the chains that bound them together.

The Wisest King Alive reached the conclusion of his speech. "During my reign, this Kingdom will enjoy an era of prosperity unseen in living memory. I give my word."

As the crowd threw themselves to the ground, Mud stormed across the Royal Square, nearly tripping several times over their prostrate forms. Frederick trailed behind, a little more discreetly.

"Bunch of bloody cretins," Mud muttered. "Wouldn't know good government if it fell from the sky."

They left the city unhampered. Everyone was too busy worshipping the Wisest King Alive to stop and question them. Standing in the outskirts of town, Mud kicked at a clump of grass. "They can have their bloody Kingdom. It's a pretty shoddy one, anyhow."

Frederick sighed. "Very well. Where do we go now?"

Mud pondered this. Then his eyes lit up. "The Northern Realm! Since King Cedric insisted on helping to take *my* Kingdom, I'll simply take his."

"That's the daftest thing I've heard all week," Frederick said. "And considering I've spent the week with you, I've heard some fairly daft things."

"Nonsense—it'll be easy. King Cedric's subjects can't possibly like him. He's a schmuck."

Frederick gave up. "Fine. I have nothing better to do. Let's travel to the Northern Realm."

*

And travel they did—for five-hundred leagues, give or take, across a barren, unforgiving desert. But that was okay. They didn't forgive it, either.

The long journey diluted their conversation somewhat. Mud had recently graduated from declaring, "I'm hungry," to announcing, "I'm skinny." He thought this a more subtle method of conveying his suffering.

Each night, when the sun went down, they would start a fire with two rocks they'd found in a canyon and then Mud would read his biography. The pages were wrinkled and smeared from constant perusal, but still legible. Desperately, he tried to make sense of the life they described. He tried to justify everything he'd done, but soon found himself justifying his justifications. The only positive thing he could say about the manuscript was that it had been written, and even that assertion was losing its merit.

After that he would join Frederick in staring into the meagre flames, Mud mourning his Kingdom, Frederick mourning Eliza and his fiddle.

They both mourned food.

In the morning, whichever of them was feeling more motivated would kick the other out of his gloomy stupor, which had become their substitute for sleep. They broke their fast—usually by sucking on the fire rocks—and set out again.

Their favourite pastime was expressing their extreme dislike for each other. They made a game of it, the object of which was to make the other resent his own existence.

"I hate you," Frederick would spontaneously affirm, initiating their daily contest.

"I hate you more," Mud would quickly retort.

"I hate you more than both our hatreds combined."

"That's mathematically unsound."

"Exactly."

Mud bristled. "My hatred for you is so strong, it enjoyed a brief existence as love before becoming an even stronger hatred."

"Yeah? Well I hate you so much, it's now my default emotion. I needed to invent a new emotion to express how much I hate you. I named it *Mud*."

For a moment, it seemed Frederick had won.

"I hate you while I'm asleep."

"I hate you while I'm *awake*."

Mud sputtered. "I hate you more than I hate picking grime from between my toes every morning!"

Frederick drew a deep breath, and then said: "I hate you more than I hate being hungry."

Mud stared at him in disbelief. "Really?"

Frederick nodded vigorously.

"Okay, you win. I'll get you tomorrow."

One night, three bandits ambushed them.

150

"Get up!" the bandit leader ordered. He brandished a rapier. "Relinquish your possessions."

Frederick regarded him queerly. "What kind of bandit uses the word 'relinquish'?"

"An educated one! Now, relinquish 'em!"

Mud and Frederick carefully laid out their belongings, which were comprised of their fire rocks and their third outfit. Mud kept his biography hidden in his shirt.

"That all?" the bandit leader said.

One of the subordinate bandits approached Mud and smacked him in his chest. A couple pages fluttered out. "What's this?"

"Oh, just a story," Mud said. "A particularly bad one, actually."

"Take it," the leader ordered his underling. "We'll use it for kindling."

Mud's face contorted. The bandit withdrew the manuscript roughly, crumpling its pages even further.

"No!" said Mud.

The bandits regarded him thoughtfully. "Um, yes," the leader replied, and that seemed to resolve the issue. They strode away into the darkness.

Without thinking, Mud seized a nearby chunk of wood and chased after them. He caught up with the leader, laying him flat with a single blow. The other two turned to face him, and Mud struck one of them in the shin, sending him hopping about and yelping.

The third bandit appraised him fearfully. "Who are you?" he said in a wavering voice.

"I am Mud!" Mud roared, and chased his adversary into the night.

He returned shortly and found Frederick sitting alone by the fire. "Where are the other two?" Mud asked him.

The fiddler continued to gaze at the dancing light. "They went off with our stuff."

"The manuscript?" Mud said.

"Scattered over there somewhere," Frederick said, pointing.

Mud scampered off and began to collect the numerous pages. He returned wearing a concerned frown. "I'm missing the part about my poker winning streak. That was my favourite."

Frederick failed utterly to commiserate.

"Do you think the Wisest King Alive will rewrite it?"

Frederick didn't answer.

Sighing, Mud took a spot near the fire.

"So, what did you think of my fight with the bandits?"

The fiddler shrugged.

"Pretty impressive, huh?"

"I guess so. I'm going to sleep."

*

Sir Forsythe moved to the corner formed by the wall and the alcove's edge, and peered carefully down the hallway. Nobody was coming. He prepared to sprint to the next alcove, but hesitated, grimacing. This would be so simple, if it weren't for...

He shook his head. He would let nothing distract him.

For the past week, he had been conducting clandestine excursions into the castle in order to spy on the new monarchy. He usually tried to avoid the mire of politics—with the exception of a recent demolition, which his honour had demanded—but something about the Wisest King Alive bothered him. Not that the new ruler was any worse than the former. But Forsythe didn't like the way he'd taken the throne, and besides, despite the former King's incompetence and depravity, the knight had grown rather fond of him.

The former King was presumed dead, but Sir Forsythe had his doubts. The knight had long suspected the man of being the gods' personal jester, and far too amusing to kill off.

Forsythe dashed for the next alcove, but was halted by a shrill, whining voice.

"Forsythe, wait! You *know* I can't run in this dress! *Wait!*"

The knight spun around. "Shut up, woman! You'll have both our heads on the chopping block!"

Countess Francine, having finally extracted herself from the alcove—almost knocking over a crystal vase in the process—stopped and stared bashfully at the floor. "I *am* sorry, Forsythe, but really, this dress—"

"I *told* you to wear something more mobile! In fact, I told you not to come at all, but you kept insisting..." He trailed off, breathing heavily. Before meeting Francine, he never let his temper get the better of him. "Listen, if we're going to do this, we have to be quiet. And we have to stop standing in the middle of the hallway."

Footsteps echoed down the corridor. Forsythe's heartbeat tripled. A guard approached.

Francine squeaked, and darted back toward the alcove.

Forsythe grabbed her. "It's too late," he whispered, "He's already seen us. Just play along."

The guard reached them. "Hey! Who are you? No one's allowed inside the castle except on royal business."

Sir Forsythe nodded. "Yes, I know. That's why I'm removing this intruder. I'm a servant, you see, and I caught this woman sneaking around."

Francine looked at him in astonishment. "But that's not true at all, For—"

"*Silence, miscreant!*" Sir Forsythe cleared his throat, shooting the guard a nervous smile. "As I was saying, I—"

"I heard what you said. But if you're a servant, then where's your livery?"

The knight hesitated, his mind racing. "Dry cleaners," he said. "Take for bloody ever, don't they?"

The guard frowned. "What's a dye clinger?"

Forsythe grimaced. He really had to stop referencing concepts he hadn't patented yet. "Listen, I'd better take this woman outside. We wouldn't want King Cedric to see her, would we? He's liable to execute the both of us. On a whim."

The guard turned white. "Cripes, you're right. Get her out of here, and don't tell anyone you were talking to me."

Sir Forsythe assured him he wouldn't, and began pulling Francine roughly down the corridor.

"Hey, wait a second!" The guard was staring hard at the knight. "Aren't you—?"

"Sir Forsythe, the famous doctor, alchemist, knight and anatomist?" Forsythe shot back. "No, he's my cousin. Resemblance is uncanny, isn't it?"

The guard nodded. "It sure is. You're a lucky guy. Handsome, that one."

The knight grinned. "Thanks." He dragged Francine away, mopping sweat from his brow.

The throne polisher paced to and fro before the cottage. The mountain breeze felt cool against his uncovered abdomen.

"I'm famished," he said.

Mud kept the chunk of wood he'd used to fight off the bandits, and spent an evening hardening it over the fire. He clubbed a wildcat with it, which was probably why he and Frederick survived. The meat lasted them a week.

Their game of hatred continued, even after Mud saved their lives.

"I wonder what we'd do if we didn't abhor each other," Mud said one morning. "Imagine if we could tolerate, or even liked each other. We'd perish from sheer boredom."

Finally the desert ended, and they reached the Northern Realm. Seeing it for the first time, Mud said, "Wow! This is my kind of Kingdom!"

The sun shone from a cloudless sky, and twin hills dominated the land. Atop one of them sat a glamorous palace.

"It's sensibly situated!" Mud said, pointing at the palace excitedly. "I can't wait to live in it!"

On the second hill, an enormous edifice was under construction. Its purpose evaded them.

Walking through the market, they noticed how sad everyone seemed, despite the excellent weather. They all exchanged goods without speaking, or making eye contact. Even the shoplifters moved sluggishly, apparently indifferent to whether the proprietors caught them or not.

"This is going to be easy!" said Mud. "Look how disenchanted everyone is with King Cedric's reign!"

A weathered man approached them. "Excuse me, but did you just say, 'King Cedric'?"

Mud hesitated. "Er, yes."

"Could you say it again?"

"Why?"

"Well, it's just that I haven't heard his name spoken since breakfast, and I quite enjoy hearing it. I'm wondering if you could see your way clear to repeating it."

"King Cedric," said Frederick. Mud scowled at him.

The man inhaled sharply, apparently savouring every syllable. "Thank you," he murmured. "Thank you. You're too kind."

Mud and Frederick exchanged glances.

Frederick changed the subject. "What's that for?" he asked, indicating the strange structure they had spotted earlier.

"Funny you should ask that," the man said. "I happen to be one of the artisans working on it. That's a giant sculpture of King Cedric—at least, it will be. We're constructing the left boot, now."

Mud's brow furrowed. "Why on Earth would you want a giant sculpture of King Cedric?"

"To honour him, of course!" The artisan paused. "Only, we've recently encountered a major problem."

"What is it?" Frederick asked, amused at Mud's distress.

"Well, we're not sure if it will be big enough."

"Not big enough!" Mud cried.

"Exactly. I mean, how do we know if we're honouring him quite enough? Regardless of how big the statue is, King Cedric will return and commend us for our work. That's the kind of guy he is. But how can one be sure one is truly imparting enough honour? There's always the danger of falling short. And what if another Kingdom builds a bigger statue, in tribute to *their* ruler? Why, ours would be as nothing. Just a big lump of wood."

"That's ludicrous!" said Mud. "That's completely ludicrous."

"You're telling me! We may have to start the entire boot over again."

Mud smouldered.

"But if you like King Cedric so much," said Frederick, "then why are people so unhappy?"

"Because he's been gone so long! Say, who are you two?"

Mud remained sullenly silent. Frederick answered for both of them. "I'm Frederick, and this is..." He trailed off for a moment, unable to suppress a snicker. "...this is Mud."

The artisan gave a start. He stared hard at the former King. "Mud?" he said. "*The* Mud?"

155

Mud frowned. "How many Muds can there possibly be?"

"*You're* Mud the Marauder? He With The Fearsome Chunk Of Wood?"

"What?" said Frederick.

The artisan's gaze happened upon the chunk of wood held loosely in Mud's hand. The man fell to his knees, and began kissing the grimy hem of Mud's robes. "It is an honour!" he cried. "Oh, what an honour!"

Mud stepped out of the man's reach. "How do you know me?"

"I've heard all about your exploits in the desert! Plundering your way through the wilderness! Striking fear in the hearts of all you encounter! I'm all aflutter!"

Other peasants drew near, wondering what all the commotion was about.

"This is Mud the Marauder!" the artisan told them. "He With The Fearsome Chunk Of Wood!"

The peasants began talking excitedly among themselves. They pointed at Mud's chunk of wood. Without warning, they hoisted Mud above their shoulders, carrying him around the marketplace and chanting.

"Mud! Mud the Marauder! He With The Fearsome Chunk Of Wood!"

Finally they set him down again, encircling and peppering him with questions.

"Have you come to rob us, Mr. Marauder? You can steal my sow! I've been fattening her up all year!"

"Will you bless my baby? Just there on the left ankle. Would you be so kind?"

"Could you steal my sister? She's annoying!"

Before long, Mud was laden with things he 'stole' from the populace. He acquired provisions, flint and steel, several clean changes of clothing, and a porcelain doll wearing a beanie. From one peasant, he 'thieved' a rucksack to carry it all in.

That night, they 'cheated' an innkeeper out of his best room.

"You can stow away there for the night," the stout man told them with a wink. "It's got two feather beds. I'll have its present occupants moved to another room."

"This is amazing," Frederick said when they were settled away. He reclined in an overstuffed armchair. "You clubbed a couple of bandits, and now you're treated like royalty."

"I *am* royalty."

"You *were* royalty."

They climbed into the spacious beds and soon drifted peacefully off. Until, that is, around three in the morning, when Mud woke up to see someone standing near the window, silhouetted by moonlight. There was something strange about the figure's outline, but Mud couldn't quite place it.

"Frederick," he whispered.

"What?" the fiddler said blearily from the other bed.

"Aren't you standing in front of that window?"

"No."

"Then who is?"

Cautiously, they lit the bedside torch. They shrieked.

It was the advisor, whose brains were oozing out from under the metal plate stitched to his skull. He stepped forward, and the plate wobbled. Its stitching had come loose.

Still screaming, Mud snatched up his new rucksack and dashed from the room. Frederick followed hastily.

*

The Wisest King Alive and Eliza stood in the throne room, staring pensively at the wall. They faced a rather unique dilemma.

"The colour definitely has to change," the new King said.

One of the first things he had done with his newfound authority was to begin renovating the royal castle. In fact, 'renovate' may be too mild a word. The castle had endured decades of neglect, and practically needed to be rebuilt. The Wisest King Alive was surprised it still stood.

"Okay," Eliza said patiently. "So what's the problem? Don't you know what colour you'll paint it?"

The Wisest King Alive paused. "Well, no. But that's not really the issue, is it? I don't feel right thinking about what colour I'm changing it *to* when I can't even figure out what colour I'm changing it *from*."

Eliza studied the wall. "I can see how that might be a problem," she said. The colour *was* difficult to classify. Neither Eliza nor the Wisest King Alive had ever encountered that particular shade before.

A rustling sound drew his attention to the corner of the throne room. Eliza had recently placed a potted fern there, and its leaves were trembling as though recently bumped.

"Did you hear that?" he said.

"Hear what?"

"I think—" he began, but stopped. He was about to say, "I think your plant just moved," but that was absurd. "Never mind," he said instead.

They turned back to the wall.

"I can't even begin to describe it," he said. "And it *is* a problem, you know. A big one. The colour a room used to be is just as significant as the colour it is presently. The *Kingdom Clarion* is doing a feature on the castle renovations, and they're bound to focus on the throne room." The *Kingdom Clarion* was a new newspaper about royal life, which the Wisest King Alive had founded. "They'll want to know what colour the throne room used to be, and what will I tell them?"

"You could lie."

The Wisest King Alive considered this. "I could, but then I'd be just as bad as my predecessor."

Eliza shrugged. "You could invent a colour. You could say the throne room was painted gloop, and when they say they've never heard of gloop, you'll tell them neither had you, before you made it up."

"Hmm. This requires extensive contemplation. I must retire to my bedchambers."

The Wisest King Alive began to leave.

"How is the manuscript coming?"

The new King tensed visibly. "It isn't," he said, and quickly left.

*

Well-made fiddles were difficult to come by, but Frederick *was* able to procure a masterfully crafted oboe—an instrument with which he was also proficient. In doing so, he earned a part in the stories that circulated about Mud the Marauder. He became Frederick the Oboist, who played up-tempo music while Mud robbed people with his chunk of wood.

Of course, Frederick started doing this only after he heard a rumour that said he did. It seemed like the sort of thing he might enjoy, and so he began doing it.

Tonight he piped merrily on his oboe as Mud hoisted himself up to an open window. The Marauder paused, and shushed Frederick. The Oboist stopped playing, and Mud pulled himself up the rest of the way.

The pair had returned to their native Kingdom, but not to the capital city. Instead they roamed the countryside, plundering the homes of willing peasants and, in doing so, increasing their fame.

They had become heroes of the people, and far more interesting than the Wisest King Alive, who was such a prudent ruler his subjects suffered from chronic boredom. No one could discern any controversy surrounding him whatsoever, other than the usurped throne upon which he sat. First they had worshipped him, but now they mostly ignored him.

Mud lowered himself carefully into what seemed to be a sitting room. Suddenly he lost his grip and crashed to the floor. He cringed, waiting for someone to come charging in.

No one came. Mud began to breathe once more. He got up and started across the room.

"Have you come to rob my family?" asked a tiny voice.

Mud spun quickly around, and spotted a lad of about four.

He sighed. "Er, yes. I have."

"I'm going to get my step-daddy!" the boy squealed, and turned to run down the hall.

Mud seized the youngster. "Not before I'm gone," he whispered.

The boy struggled in his grip. "But he's always wanted to meet you!"

The Marauder paused for a moment, and then, shrugging, released the lad. He still wasn't used to this.

"Very well. Go fetch him."

"There's some brandy in the pantry you can filch!" the boy said, and scurried off.

Mud quickly located the booze. He helped himself to a large amount of it.

The boy returned with his stepfather. "Hello, intruder," the clean-shaven man said. "Are you really Mud?"

Mud nodded. He held up his chunk of wood for inspection.

"Aha," the man said. "It vaguely resembles a striking cobra, just like in the stories."

Mud glanced down at his weapon. "A cobra? Really?"

The man extended his hand. "I'm Ralph the Nomad."

They shook. "Nice to finally meet you," said Mud.

"Pardon me?"

"Oh, I nearly had you executed, once."

"What?"

"Never mind. Hey, if you're a nomad, what are you doing living in this house? With a child?"

Ralph grimaced. "It's a long story. Perhaps you should sit down."

Mud fumbled in the dark until he found a weathered armchair. Ralph remained standing.

"A maiden of exceeding beauty had recently been widowed, and left with a child. I pitied her, so I began coming around to help her with the chores. Eventually, we married."

Mud blinked. "That wasn't a long story."

Ralph shrugged. "I'm a man of few words."

Mud poured the ex-nomad a glass of his own brandy. "In that case, let's get down to business. What do you have for me to steal?"

"Nothing, actually. I'm not letting you take anything."

The Marauder frowned. "That's not usually how it works."

"Be that as it may—I'd enjoy chatting with you, but I won't let you raid my wife's house."

There was a brief silence. "I'm sorry to hear that," said Mud, and stood up.

He stepped forward, hefting his chunk of wood threateningly. He had undergone an immense transition, these past months. He used to be a feeble, immoral tyrant with no respect for those with less power. Now he was a strong, immoral tyrant with no respect for those with less power.

Ralph shook his head. "No use, Marauder. I learned a few things in the wilderness. I could disarm you with my bare hands. As for the knife hidden up my sleeve, it could only make matters worse."

Mud reconsidered. He returned to the armchair. "Very well. What do you wish to discuss?"

"I tire of the domestic life. I wish to join you."

The former ruler whistled. Ralph *was* a man of few words.

"And what will your wife have to say?"

"Actually, I haven't quite talked it over with—"

"*I'll* tell you what I have to say!" a deep voice boomed from down the hall. The house shook as something very large approached.

A humongous woman entered the room and stood over Ralph. She stuffed her hands into her ample hips, and squinted.

"'Exceeding beauty,'" Mud murmured.

"You won't be returning to the nomadic life until you paint the fence," the hefty lady said loudly. Ralph cringed. "And what about little Tommy? He needs to learn his letters!"

"I don't want to learn my letters!" little Tommy wailed.

"I don't even know my own letters!" Ralph said.

"*Do you want I should sit on you?*"

Ralph had grown deathly pale. "Not particularly."

At this time Mud jumped up, and began tapping his faithful chunk of wood meaningfully against his leg. "Now, now, there isn't any need for sitting on anyone. Don't you know who I am?"

"An idiot with a club?" the maiden said. "Get out of my house!" She advanced toward him.

He cowered, losing some of his gall. "I'm Mud the Marauder!" he managed.

The woman drew up, reining in her bulk just in time. "Liar!" she bellowed, abusing his eardrums.

"It's true!" He showed her his chunk of wood.

Ralph's wife gasped in delight. "Really? Are you really the Marauder?"

He nodded.

"Will you autograph my pantyhose?" She began to hike up her dress. Ralph glanced at her askance.

Mud raised his eyebrows. "Madam, please release that garment."

The housewife shifted her considerable weight bashfully. "It really is a pleasure to meet you," she said, blushing.

Mud cleared his throat. "Yes, well, formalities aside. I'm here to steal your husband."

"Sincerely? I'm being robbed by Mud the Marauder?"

"That's right, madam," Mud said gravely. "And there is nothing that can be done about it."

"Oh, of course not! Of course there isn't!"

Mud grabbed Ralph and headed for the door. "I'll just be taking him, then."

"Of course you will!" she shouted after them.

Once outside, they collected Frederick and dashed across the property, leaping over the unpainted fence.

"Thanks," Ralph the recently-restored Nomad said to Mud. "She's a very flighty woman, though. She'll have her mind changed about this in another minute."

A piercing shriek emanated from the shack behind them. They ran faster.

"This is Frederick the Oboist, then?" Ralph panted.

"That's right," Frederick replied curtly, always hesitant about meeting Mud's weird friends.

"Pleasure," said Ralph.

*

King Cedric V bustled into the Wisest King Alive's study, completely throwing off his train of thought. The Wisest King Alive threw down his quill in disgust.

"What are you still doing in this Kingdom, anyway?" he snapped. He was in poor spirits. He was at an impasse with his manuscript, and the recent issue of the *Kingdom Clarion* had barely sold a hundred copies.

The visiting King stopped, looking hurt. "Gods, I'm only helping you get your reign off the ground. Besides, they're building me a monument back home. It would be rude to return during its construction."

The new King sighed. "I'm sorry for losing my temper. For what purpose have you approached me?"

162

"It's this Marauder person everyone's talking about, sire. He's trouble."

"I fail to see how. Yes, he robs people blind—but they love it. Peasants consider themselves fortunate when Mud burgles their homes. He's just some kind of twisted Santa Claus."

"He's a threat to your authority. The public knows him better than they know you."

The Wisest King Alive made a steeple with his fingers, peering at King Cedric over the top. "This is hardly a popularity contest."

"But have you heard of his traveling companion? Do you know his name?"

"Yes. It's Frederick. The *Oboist*."

"Exactly!"

"Our Frederick played the fiddle. It's a coincidence, Cedric."

The King of the Northern Realm drew himself up indignantly. Evidently, he found the Wisest King Alive's failure to use his proper title offensive.

"Very well. You shall do as you see fit, I suppose." He started to leave.

"Oh, and Cedric?"

King Cedric paused, even more indignant.

"If I discover the recent peasant disappearances are connected to you and your executioner friend, I shall have you hanged myself."

Wordlessly, King Cedric V stormed out.

*

The three men relaxed around the fire, drinking liquor and belching prodigiously. They were drinking Bloody Marys, mixed expertly by Ralph. He had learned how from his cousin.

"I'm the happiest I've ever been," declared Mud the Marauder.

"I wouldn't go back to my old life for a million pounds," added Frederick the Oboist.

"I'm thinking about divorcing my wife," said Ralph the Nomad.

"My brains are oozing out my ears," said the advisor.

The other three jumped up, and stared in horror at the monstrosity now sitting with them at the fire.

Mud broke the silence. "That's it. I'm putting an end to this. Hand me my chunk of wood." Frederick did, and Mud advanced around the fire toward his old advisor.

The advisor also stood, and approached Mud with his shuffling step. He held his arms out, groping in the dark. His condition had seriously worsened since last Mud saw him. Brains really *did* leak out his ears, and his eyes protruded slightly from his head. Mud brought his chunk of wood back intending to put the abomination out of its misery.

"Mud, wait!" Ralph the Nomad shouted.

Mud stayed his hand. "Why?" he and Frederick demanded in unison.

Ralph swallowed. "I think I recognize this man."

Mud was going to protest, but thought better of it. He sighed. "Fine. If we're not going to kill him, then we better flee."

They ran from the fire screaming.

*

"Why didn't you let me finally slay him?" Mud said the next morning. "He's been haunting me for far too long."

For a long while, Ralph didn't answer. Finally, he said, "I don't know quite how to say this, but the man you nearly killed last night is my wife's deceased husband. I recognize him from family portraits."

Mud scratched his head. "But you clearly knew exactly how to say it."

Ralph opened his mouth, but Mud forestalled him. "Never mind. Explain what you just said."

Ralph nodded. "In life, he was rarely ever seen by his wife. He had an important government job in town. One day she received word he died, and had been given a decent burial."

"I didn't even know he was married," Mud said.

Each man perused his confused thoughts.

"I might have a solution," Frederick said.

The next time the advisor showed up at their campfire, they threw him in a sack and brought him to Ralph's old house.

"So you see," the Nomad said to his ex-wife, "I can't be your husband, because your original spouse is still alive and...uh, well."

164

A long silence prevailed. The robust housewife eyed the undead advisor in shock. Her old husband was standing with the help of Frederick, who eyed the gray matter oozing from beneath the metal plate. Her mouth quivered. Finally, she spoke.

"Darling, have you lost weight?"

The advisor gurgled, no longer capable of normal speech. Mud doubted this mattered much, as his wife seemed perfectly able to hold up both ends of the conversation.

Mud approached his old advisor and shook his withered hand. He hesitated, and then said, "It's been a pleasure working with you." The words felt foreign in his mouth.

Something seemed to register in the advisor's goggling eyes. He raised a clumsy limb and dropped it onto Mud's shoulder, in a gesture vaguely redolent of companionship. Mud smiled feebly and pulled away, shuddering.

"Mud?" Ralph said. "You were also acquainted with this man? Is there something you aren't telling me?"

"Yes. There is. And I'll tell you it when we're drunker."

*

The Wisest King Alive was in disguise. He wore a hooded robe, and his beard was tucked neatly inside. Shadows hid his face. He'd read about other rulers who concealed their identity to walk among the public, gauging their mood. That's what the Wisest King Alive was doing. He doubted even Eliza would recognize him.

"Morning, Your Majesty," said a passing peasant.

The Wisest King Alive frowned after the man. "Who?" he said weakly.

The peasant shot a knowing smile over his shoulder.

The monarch approached a produce stand, straining to be nonchalant. "Good day. I would like a pomegranate, to go with my commoner's breakfast."

The proprietor raised an eyebrow. "Sorry, but we don't get that kind of exotic import here."

The Wisest King Alive cleared his throat. "Of course not. I was merely joking. Ha, ha."

"They have them in the castle, though. Why didn't you just eat one there, sire?"

The Wisest King Alive's throat constricted. "I don't know what you're..."

He trailed off, as both his attention and the shopkeeper's were drawn to a well-dressed man, who sidled toward the produce stand. Suddenly the man snatched an apple and ran off with it, whooping.

"Good morning!" the shopkeeper cried, waving after him.

The Wisest King Alive furrowed his brow. "That man just robbed you."

The proprietor nodded, beaming. "Yes, charming, isn't it?"

"Aren't you going to do anything?"

"Of course not! Why would I?"

"But he just *robbed* you!"

"I know that. Haven't you heard of Mud the Marauder?"

"I've heard of him, yes..."

"He's made stealing the next big thing. It's become a sign of respect and well-meaning." The shopkeeper's grin broadened. "My shop is one of the most frequently stolen from."

"But don't you find that at all unpleasant?"

"Well, it's a little bad for business, yes, but there's no reason to be a poor sport about it."

The Wisest King Alive looked around the marketplace with new eyes. He realized that everywhere, people were pilfering from shops and from each other. The place was in utter chaos.

He felt a tug at his own pocket. "Cut that out!" he yelled at the urchin trying to filch his money pouch. The lad scowled, and ran off to pick someone else's pocket.

"I've got to do something about this," he muttered.

"Oh, there's nothing to be done about it," the shopkeeper said. "Mud is far too revered for it to stop anytime soon. Did you know he found his famed chunk of wood in the desert? Who but Mud could find wood in the desert?" He chuckled.

The Wisest King Alive bid the shopkeeper a hasty farewell, and hurried back to the castle. Once there he leapt into his bed, and hid.

*

Mud reclined on the jagged fireside rock and thought about how much more comfortable it was than his throne. On reflection, the artisan responsible for crafting his former royal perch couldn't have been very familiar with how a human body was shaped.

In fact, many aspects of his reign had bothered him, and he only realized it now. He hated being pestered constantly, he hated his shabby old castle, and most of all, he hated responsibility. Or at least, he hated the little responsibility he had chosen to take on.

As well, people had never really viewed his existence in a positive light until he changed his name to Mud.

He still wanted his throne back, of course.

They met many people during their travels, most who were admirers of Mud the Marauder. Because of their lengthy titles, introductions consumed a lot of their time. They took to gathering everyone in one place before divulging their names, and anyone absent would just have to do without.

Most were admirers of Mud, but many knew of his skill in battle and wished to duel him. He became quite adept at avoiding such contests, however some were unavoidable—especially when the challenger was the offspring of some powerful local noble. Mud's companions were no help. Frederick the Oboist didn't know one end of a chunk of wood from the other, and Ralph the Nomad, despite his alleged skill in martial arts, was usually content to sit by and watch. They both found Mud's reluctance to fight extremely entertaining.

Once, as they strolled down a secluded country road, Mud was struck unconscious by a rock. He awoke to find bandits surrounding him, with Ralph and Frederick tied up nearby.

The leader spoke. It was the same bandit that tried to take Mud's manuscript, when they first started traveling.

"Are you Mud the Marauder?" he asked. Mud's appearance had changed since their last meeting, and the bandit leader seemed unsure.

While Mud contemplated which answer would be most conducive to his survival, Ralph replied for him: "He sure is Mud the Marauder, and you'd better treat him with respect!"

A bandit beaned him with a rock, and he fell forward onto his face.

The leader grabbed Mud by the lapels. "We've got a bone to pick with you," he growled.

Frederick arched an eyebrow. "A bone to pick? Isn't that a little clichéd?" He shook his head in disappointment. "And I thought you were an educated bandit."

Which earned Frederick a rock across the skull, too.

"We don't like your style," the bandit leader said to Mud. "Taking things from people because they worship you isn't banditry—it's religion."

Mud considered this. "Debateable."

"Wrong," said the bandit leader, punctuating the syllable with a sharp slap. Mud reeled, but the bandit drew him closer. "Debate is something held in courts, not on your knees by the side of the road."

Mud's head throbbed. He glanced about discreetly for his chunk of wood.

The bandit leader continued. He seemed to enjoy hearing himself speak. "We bandits have always worked hard for our bounty. No one ever *gave* it to us. That isn't how it works." He glanced disdainfully at Frederick, who was still unconscious. "And to hang around with a clarinet player—"

"Oboe player," Mud corrected him.

"What?"

"He plays the oboe."

"Oh," said the bandit leader. In spite of himself, a note of interest crept into his voice. "I've never heard of one of those."

"You haven't?" said Mud, who hadn't either, before he'd met Frederick. "They're rather popular, nowadays."

For the first time, a bandit other than the leader spoke. "And what does he do with it?"

"He plays it while I rob folks with my chunk of wood."

The bandit leader's eyebrows shot up, and the others whispered amongst themselves.

One cleared his throat. "A chunk of wood?"

"You haven't heard the legend?"

"Someone started to tell me, but I punched him out."

Mud smiled. He had finally spotted his weapon. "That," he said with emphasis, "is my chunk of wood."

The others followed his gaze to where the chunk of wood lay, a short distance from the road.

"You rob people with *that?*" the leader asked. He swallowed. "That's pretty impressive."

The others nodded in agreement.

Ten minutes later Mud, Frederick and Ralph exchanged farewells with the bandits, and rode off on the horses their new friends 'relinquished'.

"I'm naming mine the Prince," said Mud.

The rumours surrounding Mud the Marauder were soon altered to accommodate the horse.

Mud discovered the more they journeyed, the more his relationship with Frederick improved. It cooled from searing hatred to simmering dislike. He no longer feared the Oboist would kill him, especially considering Mud's newfound prowess with the chunk of wood. And Frederick, it seemed, had cultivated a begrudging respect for the Marauder.

Life—that abstract concept which defies definition—eased itself into a comfortable routine. In truth, Mud was prepared to procrastinate retaking his throne indefinitely.

And then he met Linus.

It began as a regular roadside mugging. Mud, Ralph and Frederick awkwardly ignored their victim's jubilation at being robbed by Mud the Marauder while they relieved him of his belongings. Except, as Mud soon noticed, the man wasn't at all jubilant. He was staring at Mud's face in utter astonishment.

"Your Majesty?" he said wonderingly.

"Where?" Ralph asked, looking about fearfully. The Nomad possessed a keen paranoia of authority.

"You have the wrong man," Mud assured him.

Their victim nodded. "You were always the wrong man, sire. Nevertheless, you *are* the former King."

Ralph shot Mud a surprised look. "You are?"

"Of course he is," said Frederick. "Haven't I ever mentioned?"

"Okay!" Mud cried, waving his hands for order. "Okay. I think we'd better dip into the brandy."

Linus, they learned once they'd all been equipped with a mug, was a member of the now defunct Traveling Linguists' Guild. "We were all exiled from town by that wanker, King Cedric. Scattered in all directions, with our leader beheaded—not that that's a particularly bad thing. Anyway, I ran into a few mates on the road, and we're thinking about getting the Guild back together." He paused to sip his brandy. "You remember that tribe Larry wanted executed? The one whose language causes them to hyperventilate? That's where I'm headed now. I'm planning to modify the unified theory to accommodate them."

Mud mulled this over. Too casually, he said, "This tribe you speak of. Is it...warlike?"

"Oh, not at all. They're rather a placid folk. They lead a very simple life."

"I see. Do you mind if we accompany you?"

"Well, no. Not really. It'll be fairly dull, though. Their language is complex, and terribly slow-paced."

"But you do speak it?"

Linus nodded.

Mud shot his two traveling companions a firm look. "It's settled, then. We're going."

The next issue that needed settling was Ralph's mounting confusion concerning Mud's identity. The obvious remedy was to get obscenely drunk, and that's exactly what they did.

*

"I don't care what colour napkins we have at the bloody reception!" the Wisest King Alive shouted.

Eliza stood in the doorway, holding a turquoise napkin in one hand and a fuchsia one in the other. She looked hurt.

A sudden *snap* filled the room. He had broken his quill.

Eliza began to weep, using the turquoise napkin to dry her eyes. The Wisest King Alive realized how insensitive he was being, and walked over to her.

"I guess we'll have to go with fuchsia now, hmm?" he said. He tried to embrace her.

She pulled away from him. "You've been impossible ever since you began work on that manuscript again."

170

He sighed. "I'm sorry, dearest. It's just I'm suffering from an insurmountable bout of writer's block. Kind of inevitable, I suppose, considering my subject has been presumed dead. I just wish I had the first half of the manuscript."

Eliza wiped her eyes again. "It's okay." She changed the subject. "Honey, that reminds me. I was wondering: have you heard yet from the throne polisher? He's been gone for a while, now."

"You're right. I should probably send someone after him." He paused. "Listen, sweetcake. I'm sorry I've been such a buffoon. Writing a biography and being King are two endeavours that don't really coincide."

She embraced him. "I understand. Perhaps we should have just stayed on Mount High."

The Wisest King Alive stroked her hair. He just barely stopped himself from agreeing.

The moment was interrupted by a crashing sound from just outside the study. "Blast, woman!" said a male voice. "Run!" Twin footsteps receded quickly down the hall.

Eliza and the Wisest King Alive hurried to the door. Outside, an expensive marble statue had been upset from its pedestal, and was now badly chipped.

The Wisest King Alive frowned. "Alice, have you noticed how nosy the servants are becoming?"

*

A river burbled nearby, and it sounded very similar to the noises coming from the native with whom Mud now spoke. The long-haired man finished his sentence, and, having hyperventilated, promptly passed out.

Linus translated: "He says, 'To to around within to to on top of between.'"

Mud stared. "And that means…"

"The rough translation is this: 'Welcome to our humble riverside home. Please feel free to look around. We will do everything within our power to ensure your stay is pleasurable. If you care to meet her, our leader and guardian resides on top of the nearby mountain.' Er, he also expressed a philosophical notion he's been meaning to communicate, but hasn't had enough breath; something about a man's soul residing between his mind and his body."

"How exactly is he able to say all that?"

"Their language relies heavily on intonation. The inflection used to speak a single preposition carries a whole sentence's worth of meaning."

"And how long will he be out?"

"A good ten minutes or so. Then he'll probably go to bed."

Mud shook his head. "Wow. So speaking is a real trial for them, huh?"

Linus nodded. "They rarely do it." He paused. "Which may explain why they get along with each other so well."

Walking around the camp, Mud could see the natives lived uncomplicated lives. They resided in modest mud huts, and played with acorns and leaves—things they found in nature. The adults frolicked alongside their children, without inhibitions. They never seemed to squabble.

Despite their healthily round stomachs, Mud couldn't find any weapons for hunting in the camp. He asked Linus about it.

"They never kill anything, ever," the linguist said. "Even picking berries from a bush is a crime worthy of banishment. They hold a deep respect for all living things."

Mud frowned. "That's all very well—very bighearted—but how are they supposed to live?"

"Well, usually one member of every generation realizes how foolish they're all being, and kills something to eat. He or she is cast out, of course, and then turns to a life of hunting and gathering. The current exile is the woman our friend mentioned earlier, who lives in a cave on the nearby mountain. She hunts for the entire tribe, cooking the food until it bears no resemblance to anything living. Then she feeds it to them. Eventually the tribe forgot having ever punished her, and began revering her as their leader. But by then she was too different to live among them, and she opted to stay up in her cave."

"She must be a formidable woman."

"Yes, and a very lonely one."

For a time, they reflected solemnly on her selfless existence. Their contemplation was interrupted by Ralph and Frederick, who approached them grinning broadly.

172

"This is amazing!" Ralph exclaimed. He had grown a beard since leaving his ex-wife, and it was currently drenched in alcohol. "Their drink is the strongest I've ever enjoyed—and *my* brother is best friends with a bartender!" He took a swig from the crude wooden mug he was holding. "And their women! The most flirtatious I've ever encountered! I can see already this will be a memorable night."

Linus walked over and slapped him. "Stay away from their women, do you hear me? You come from a far more civilized society—the concept of family doesn't even exist in theirs. If I catch you taking advantage of that fact, I will see you dead."

Ralph blinked and rubbed his face. He strode off to sit sullenly by the river.

"The same goes for you, Oboist," Linus said.

Frederick brought his oboe to his mouth and piped a dejected tune. "Musician's honour," he said, and went to join Ralph.

Linus turned to confront Mud. The Marauder held up a hand soothingly. "I'll keep an eye on my friends. The natives' purity will not be tainted by our presence."

The linguist cleared his throat. "Er, they *aren't* pure, actually, in any sense of the word. I just don't want those two muddying the gene pool."

Mud enjoyed living among the natives. They came to recognize him by his chunk of wood, and smiled amiably whenever he passed—their equivalent to a raucous cheer. After the initial welcome, however, they rarely spoke to him. Occasionally a native would offer a scattered preposition, after which he or she would have to sit down and rest.

He came to learn that 'before', spoken with rising intonation, meant, "Are you taking a swim before breakfast?" and 'without', spoken flatly, meant, "May you never go without sunshine or a bath." This was a popular saying among the natives.

"How long do they live?" Mud asked Linus as they were lounging near the riverbank.

"It depends on how talkative they are. The most loquacious die before they hit thirty, while those who speak only annually live longer than most civilized people. There's a lesson there for people in our own society, I think."

On their fourth night, the leader of the tribe approached the camp.

She bellowed so everyone present could hear, and Linus quietly translated for Mud: "Since of beneath beside across outside during instead of like before."

"Doesn't it tax her to shout so?" Mud asked the linguist.

"She's the strongest of them," said Linus, "though she will have reached her limits after that utterance."

"What did she say?"

"She said, 'I have been foraging since sunset of two days ago. I crept beneath the giant oak, I strode beside the big rock, I stalked across the great river. I left the food just outside the camp. Please eat only during mealtimes, instead of gorging yourselves incessantly like you usually do. I will return before three sunsets have passed.'"

The leader began to leave the camp, but noticed Linus and the other newcomers. She walked over and studied them a long time. Finally she looked directly at Mud and said something.

Linus translated: "She said, 'Into.'"

Suddenly the leader fell over, unconscious.

The natives panicked, scurrying to surround her. They shook her, moaning wordlessly. Those unable to reach her began to tear at their hair.

"What's all this?" Mud asked. "Why are they so worked up?"

Linus swallowed. "Their leader has never fainted before. Always, she has been able to say what she wished while remaining conscious."

"What did she say?"

The linguist winced, hesitating.

"What did she say, Linus?"

"She said, 'I enjoy looking into your eyes.'"

Mud stared hard at the unconscious woman slumped on the ground. "I like looking at you, too," he murmured.

*

Forsythe sat before the roaring fire, hardening arrowheads. He made his arrows himself. In fact, he forged all his own weapons, as well as his armour—the local blacksmith was very accommodating, allowing the knight to use his equipment whenever he wished.

Forsythe would have gone into the business himself, except as it was he rather had too many—well, let's not get into that right now.

The knight was finished with his excursions into the castle. Partly because he would suffer a heart attack if Francine knocked over one more priceless artefact, but mostly because he'd heard enough. The Wisest King Alive might have been passable as a sage, but as a ruler, he was terrible. He was obsessed with writing, interior decorating and his own upcoming wedding. Since his coronation, crime had quadrupled. The Kingdom would have been better served with the former King's goat on the throne.

Forsythe brought the tongs close, studying the glowing arrowhead. He nodded. This would be the one.

*

After the natives carried their leader to her cave, Linus rounded on Mud. "You mustn't go near her. If she were to take a mate, it would distract her from the hunt. She needs every available minute to feed the tribe."

Mud rolled his eyes.

"This is serious, Mud. It would topple their entire culture. The world has never seen anything like these natives, and probably never will again. Heed my words."

Mud coughed. "But wouldn't it be a good thing for the Guild if their culture did topple? I mean, wouldn't your unified theory thingy finally be all right, then?"

"Listen, I'm not Larry. I don't believe in restructuring the world to match my creation—I believe in restructuring my creation to match the world. This culture is a natural phenomenon. Do—not—ruin it."

Mud ground his chunk of wood in the dirt. "Fine," he muttered.

"Promise me."

"I promise."

"Give me your solemn word as the Marauder you won't go near this tribe's leader, under any circumstances."

Mud sighed. "I give my solemn word as the Marauder I won't…do what you said not to."

"A man's word defines his worth."

"You think I don't know that?"

"Very well," the linguist said, and left. Mud stared thoughtfully at his retreating back.

That night, when everyone was asleep, he snuck out of camp.

The nearby mountain hardly approached the size of Mount High, though scaling it was still quite an undertaking. Having seen the tribe's leader, however, he wasn't at all surprised she did it daily. Finally he reached a sizable opening, partially hidden by the mountain's uneven slopes.

He entered cautiously.

Immediately a blunt object connected with the back of his head, and he reeled forward into darkness.

*

He awoke some time later, with the tribal leader crouched in front of him. When he opened his eyes she gave a relieved sigh, and patted his hair apologetically. He managed a smile.

They exchanged grunts, and she showed him around her cave. She had made quite a home of it. There were animal skins to sit on, a shallow pit for having fires, and a hollow in which foodstuffs were stored. On one wall hung an extensive collection of clubs—rounded, spiked, two-handed and hooked.

"That's very impressive," said Mud. "Your prey must hate to hear you come."

She gave a gratified hum. "Upon before," she murmured.

From the little he knew of their language, Mud knew this meant, "I'm upon them before they can hear me."

She showed him the rest of her humble cave—there was a connecting room, with a bearskin laid out for a bed—and finally they rested on some animal skins placed near the fire.

"How is it you understand English?" he asked her.

"To," she rejoined softly. ("I listen to the linguists, who come often.")

"Doesn't it limit what you can communicate, speaking only in prepositions? What if you wanted to say, 'Pass the salt'? There aren't any prepositions there."

"For," she answered. ("We exchange diversity for efficiency.")

"But it isn't very efficient to hyperventilate all the time!"

176

His new friend had grew weary, however, and gave no reply. For an hour they sat in silence, simply looking at each other. To Mud's surprise, this wasn't awkward at all.

Finally, he stood up to leave. "Above to," he uttered clumsily.

She understood his meaning: "Above all, I'd like to see you soon."

The tribal leader also stood. Without warning she seized his hair, and kissed him roughly.

Finally Mud drew away, feeling dazed. He smiled, and left the cave. His dopey grin accompanied him down the mountain.

*

King Cedric brooded on his humongous, bejewelled throne. He heard someone enter, but it was too dark in the dingy chamber to discern who. The Wisest King Alive made him relocate his throne, from the throne room to the castle's dank basements, which lay below even the dungeon. Now he visited the throne in his blackest moods.

"Who is it?" he barked. A dim outline drew near, and became the captain of the forces King Cedric had brought from the Northern Realm. "Oh, it's you. What do you have to report?" The monarch gave him a look that said he'd better have *something*.

"The word has been spread to the men, Your Majesty. They know what they must do."

"Excellent," said King Cedric, and allowed himself a little giggle. Things were looking up. "And you told them to wait until after the vows, didn't you, Captain? I want to give him at least a *taste* of married life." King Cedric giggled again.

The captain's hand twitched, but he stood firm. "I did, Your Majesty."

"Exemplary. Now, leave."

The captain turned to go. He stopped, and now his distaste was plain. "Your Majesty?"

"Yes, Captain?"

The captain hesitated, and then said in a rush: "The royal executioner awaits you in the outskirts of town, with your next…prisoner."

The captain left, and King Cedric's glee at the news was tarnished by the captain's odd behaviour. The relationship between monarch and officer used to be so good—what went wrong?

No matter. The plan was well underway. Soon, this Kingdom would enjoy a new king. A real king.

It wasn't that King Cedric didn't like its current monarch. He was a decent fellow, all things considered. But did he have to go about calling himself the Wisest 'King' Alive? Claiming to be the Wisest 'Man' was arrogant enough, but the new title was basically a direct insult.

Besides, King Cedric rather liked the idea of ruling two kingdoms. Perhaps he would combine them into one realm; call it 'Cedricland'. Perhaps he could charge admission.

He would need more statues, of course. Bigger statues. Yes, the one currently under construction in the Northern Realm would have to be begun anew. But his subjects there would understand. *They*, at least, loved him.

King Cedric giggled.

*

Mud had left his heart in the tribal leader's cave. Each night he returned to fetch it, but he kept getting distracted by the huntress' wild beauty. And each night, he forgot once more to take it with him when he left.

He learned that in the tribe's language, names had no prepositions. By asking around, he discovered the leader's name was "She Who Acts Naturally." The natives usually used the abbreviated version, however: Swan.

One night he descended the slopes to find a very ticked off Linus waiting for him at the bottom.

"You've been courting the leader, haven't you?"

Mud looked at him blankly. "Yes, that's quite obvious, isn't it?"

The linguist clenched his fists. "You'll bring ruin to the entire tribe."

"Why are you such a prude? What have you got against love?"

"What have you got against cultural endurance!" Linus retorted, and stalked away.

Mud soon learned to speak the tribe's language almost fluently. His conversations with Swan didn't last very long, but they were crammed with significance. Every night, he told her another portion of his story—how he used to be King, and how he squandered the throne in his folly. Just as she grew to love Mud, she also fell in love with his tale. And, by association, his royal cause.

Every night, Mud saw her collection of clubs had increased since his last visit. She was adding new ones at a rate of two or three a day. After a week, twenty new clubs hung on the wall. There was a total of forty-two.

To all appearances, Frederick and Ralph continued to abide by Linus's wishes. They spent their days drinking and fishing by the river. As a result, they were shunned by the natives for what they saw as heinous slaughter.

Linus continued his study of the natives, diligently tweaking the Guild's unified theory. He also continued to glower at Mud, but the Marauder was much too in love to notice.

What Mud *did* notice was that the natives were slowly becoming less cordial. They rarely played with acorns anymore, and occasionally he spotted a native strutting proudly through the camp—something he hadn't seen before. Once, when it rained, the women gathered around the puddles and studied their reflections.

On one overcast morning, the grim truth came out. Inside the mud hut he'd built for himself, Mud jerked awake. He had been roused by someone's agonized scream. He scampered out. It was Linus.

A native lay at the linguist's feet. For a confused moment, Mud thought Linus had struck him. But then he saw that in one hand, the unconscious native clutched one of Swan's clubs.

He walked over. "What's going on?"

Linus seized his lapel and shook him violently. *"I'll tell you what's going on!"*

Mud stepped back, and brushed himself off. Finally he said, "Well?"

"I found this native holding a club! I demanded an explanation! Do you know what he told me?"

"No."

"He said, 'From in of past except on to with!' Then he fainted!"

The Marauder tried to work out the meaning, and failed.

"It means, 'I received this club from Swan, who has been training us in the art of club-wielding for the past month. Except on Tuesdays, when she teaches us to fight with our hands.'"

Mud nodded. "I see."

"She's training them for war!"

"Which war?" Mud asked.

He knew perfectly well which war.

Linus shook his head. "I don't know yet, but I bet it's your fault!"

"That's crazy!"

In fact, it was completely reasonable.

Unable to control his rage, Linus punched Mud in his face. Or rather, he *would* have punched Mud in the face, had the Marauder's chunk of wood not intercepted the blow.

"Listen, Linus," said Mud. "I respect your discipline, and I appreciate that your actions are in the good name of science. But I don't really understand it. All I've ever understood is what I wanted. And as King, I was usually able to get it. Since being usurped, I've had to learn new ways to satisfy myself. Inventive ways. That's a big thing for me, and I'm not going to let you ruin it. Okay?"

The linguist grimaced in disgust, and swung with the other fist. Mud had no choice but to knock Linus out and deposit him in the nearby river. And that's what he did.

Mud made his way to Swan's cave and found her studying a new club proudly. "For to," he said, meaning: "Thank you for raising an army. You didn't have to do that."

Of course, Mud was delighted she had.

*

It took Sir Forsythe all morning to find a rooftop that would afford him a clear shot. He had to be facing the Royal Square, as well as facing away from the sun. When he finally found one it was past noon, and the sun was shining in the opposite direction. He cursed.

As usual, Francine wasn't helping. "Ooh, how about that one? It's got pretty ornaments on it. Why don't you ever buy me any pretty ornaments?"

"Because you aren't my wife," he snapped.

180

He immediately regretted it. Francine's lip trembled, but luckily her attention was again diverted. "Ooh, how about that one?"

As it turned out, he ended up choosing the roof with the ornaments. Once there, he nocked his chosen arrow, and crouched against the low wall that bordered it. Francine played with a pink windmill nearby.

"Get down!" he hissed.

She sat beside him, her head still clearly visible to those now gathering in the Square. He sighed.

"Now what?" she asked.

"We wait."

*

The Wisest King Alive buttoned his tuxedo lethargically. His beard flowed absurdly over the front.

"Tuck it back like this," Eliza suggested. She had been fussing with his facial hair for the past hour.

"Are we sure we want to do this?" he said. "I mean, is marriage really for us? What if we have kids? Imagine the jokes people will make. 'Hey, look, there go the Wisest Kids Alive!' And supposing we get a cat? The margin for ridicule is overwhelming."

"These last minute worries are to be expected. Everybody has them before their wedding."

The Wisest King Alive paused. "Then why don't you have any?"

King Cedric entered the room. "Everyone is assembled in the Royal Square, oh Wisest King. Everything is prepared." Strangely, he giggled. "We await only you and your bride. Er, aren't the bride and groom supposed to be kept separate?"

"We couldn't bear to be apart," said Eliza. The Wisest King Alive shrugged uneasily.

"A good sign, I think," said King Cedric, and began rubbing his hands together vigorously. The Wisest King Alive eyed him askance. He hadn't expected Cedric to be so excited for him.

They made their way out of the castle and through the town streets. The Wisest King Alive felt like he was heading for the gallows.

"Who will be performing the wedding, King Cedric?" he asked, struggling to keep his voice level.

"The royal executioner."

The Wisest King Alive felt sweat drip from his nose and into his beard.

The Royal Square was only half full. Most peasants opted to stay at home, and the few that were present raised a half-hearted cheer at the arrival of the bride and groom. King Cedric's entourage was also there, in its entirety.

An aisle was cleared down the center of the Square. At its end stood Earl, wearing his black executioner's hood.

"Is that really necessary?" the Wisest King Alive asked King Cedric. Eliza had already begun her walk up the aisle.

"He was nervous," Cedric said. "He's never done a wedding before. For him, the hood is like a security blanket."

Finally it was the Wisest King Alive's turn to walk. He began shuffling reluctantly toward the executioner, his many years weighing heavily on him. He didn't feel very wise at all. He felt as ignorant as the basest commoner. The basest commoner's dog.

And so it was almost a relief when the former King charged into the Square, accompanied by a horde of screaming, club-wielding savages.

*

Forsythe blinked.

"What in *blazes?*" He considered shooting the Wisest King Alive anyway, but now there was no need. He stood up, and threw down his bow in disgust.

Francine embraced him, murmuring soothingly. For once, he didn't resist.

"I guess that's what I get for letting myself become involved in politics."

"What do you get?"

"Nothing at all."

*

The gathered peasants quickly fled, indifferent to who won but very concerned for their own physical wellbeing. All of King Cedric's soldiers were in attendance, however. They looked at their king, who shrugged. And so the soldiers rushed forward, having had no one to fight in months.

Ralph the Nomad was among the first to expire. It turned out he wasn't much of a fighter, after all. Many followed, and the battleground quickly turned bloody. The natives were zealous in their loyalty to Swan, and Swan was zealous in her love of Mud. The enthusiasm shown by King Cedric's soldiers soon turned to dread.

The Wisest King Alive and Eliza huddled together in the center of the square, protected by the executioner. Earl, though weaponless, began throttling enemies with his bare hands.

As for the former King, his competence in combat was astounding. Mercilessly felling foes, he rode a wild-eyed stallion, and wielded some kind of mace, or a club, or perhaps a...

The Wisest King Alive blinked. "Good gods. He's Mud the Marauder."

Suddenly he noticed an eerie tune was playing, lending grace to the clash of steel and wood. The battle became a dance, with the warriors meeting and parting to a haunting melody. The Wisest King Alive looked around for the source of the music. It was Frederick, piping on an oboe at a safe distance.

"I should have known," Eliza spat. "If anyone was going to crash my wedding, it would be him."

The battle was soon decided. King Cedric's soldiers scattered before the fearsome might of the club-wielders, and four people were captured: the Wisest King Alive, King Cedric, Eliza, and one of the bridesmaids.

Naturally, the executioner had been far too formidable a fighter to be taken prisoner. He had perished while strangling two enemies at once, after sustaining a final club wound to the head.

The former King approached the group, attended by Frederick as well as a beautiful, hale woman.

"I am Mud the Marauder," he said, "and I have come to reclaim my rightful place as—"

"Er, Mud?"

"Yes, Frederick?"

183

"You don't need to call yourself that anymore."

"Oh, that's right. I'd forgotten." He stopped for a moment, as if unsure how to proceed. "Right. I am the King," he said, "and I am here to reclaim my throne."

The Wisest King—er, Man—Alive felt relieved of a great burden. "Thank you, Your Majesty. I really didn't want it anymore." He turned to Eliza. "Listen, darling. I've been a bachelor for nearly a century now. It's taking me a while to get used to the idea of marriage. Can we postpone the wedding two or three years?"

Eliza nodded. "Of course. Being together is what's most important."

The King interrupted. "You can be together on the gallows." He paused. Everyone stared at him in shock. "Right before you die," he added.

The Wisest Man Alive regarded him incredulously. "You monster! You'd really order us executed after such a tender moment as that?"

"Yes," said the King, "I would. Unless you finish this." He handed over a wad of wrinkled pages.

"Why, it's the first half of my manuscript!"

The King nodded. "And I want you to write the second half. I'll fill in any details you're missing."

Eliza and the Wisest Man Alive entered a joyous embrace. Nearby, Frederick seethed.

Suddenly the bridesmaid tore her veil away, revealing a very pretty face underneath. The King gaped.

"*Alice?*"

She blew him a kiss teasingly. "That's right, Your Majesty."

Frederick was eyeing her in a way that was anything but subtle. "Hey, you're really good-looking."

The King held up a hand warningly. "Don't even think about it, Oboist. That's very tender emotional ground. It would uproot very painful memories if you were to...." He trailed off. Frederick wasn't listening. In fact, he and Alice had already left the Royal Square, and were heading for her place two streets over.

The reinstated monarch frowned. He sighed, and turned to King Cedric V. "You know what? You're a much better King than I am. I'm finally prepared to admit that. They're building a humongous monument in your honour in the Northern Realm, and I think you should go appreciate it. Right away." He waited. When Cedric showed no sign of moving, he said, "You may take what remains of your staff and leave."

King Cedric wavered uncertainly. He glanced from the Wisest Man Alive to the King, and back again. He glanced at the legions of scowling natives. Finally he nodded, as if to himself, and left the Square at a headlong dash.

His entourage shuffled their collective feet. "Um, we're going to stay, if that's all right," said a chef. The King nodded. He drew himself up, surveying his surroundings proudly. This was, without a doubt, his finest hour. He was glad he'd lost his throne, if only because retaking it proved so satisfying.

A distant drum roll began, punctuating his triumph. He tilted his head, smiling. The rhythmic patter grew louder.

"Where is that coming from?" he wondered aloud.

Suddenly, a swiftly-moving blur barrelled into the Square from between two peasant hovels. The King squinted at it. A moment later, he gaped.

It was his mother, riding his goat. They were headed directly for him.

He woke hours later, in the royal bedchambers, aching everywhere.

*

Linus pulled himself up onto the riverbank, dripping.

*

The Wisest Man Alive recorded everything, right up to the disrupted wedding and the King's restoration. He insisted his manuscript wasn't completed yet, however. He sensed there yet remained at least one chapter of the King's life that deserved to be documented.

Upon hearing this, the King groaned. He grew weary of doing things worth writing about.

Elizabeth the linguist was freed from the dungeon. She treated the King with indifference until she left, intent on reviving the Traveling

Linguists' Guild. Shortly after her departure Linus arrived at the castle, and now spent most of his free time berating the King.

"The natives have become civilized, sire, and it's all your fault. They speak English fluently, they drink, they quarrel, and they live in houses. I hope you're happy."

"I'm really not," the King promised.

He had everything he wanted. The castle was looking better than ever, as it enjoyed extreme renovations during the reign of the Wisest Man Alive. King Cedric had been banished. The King had regained his throne. And someone was writing his biography.

Still, he was not content.

He missed his days as Mud the Marauder, the fearsome crook who was loved by all. The public had become disenchanted with Mud the minute they discovered his true identity, and the stories quickly dissipated. Now they spoke of Gertrude the Goat Rider, who roamed the desert plains at night and brought swift wrath down upon those who refused to iron their clothes.

Public opinion of the King returned to its original dismal state. He thanked the gods the Kingdom Crier was no longer around.

What he missed most was the independence and solitude his days as the Marauder had afforded him. Every waking moment, Swan was with him. She spoke English now, and though she continued to be very concise, she was still capable of talking for hours. They walked together, they ate together, and they brushed their teeth together. Swan was a fine girl, except that she wouldn't leave him alone for more than five minutes.

He came to realize he wasn't cut out for love. His substandard personality simply wasn't compatible with that of anyone else. It was unfortunate he discovered this only after entering a serious relationship with Swan.

"I've got to have her assassinated," he decided one morning, and that was that.

*

The natives took well to civilization—so well, in fact, the civilized people looked at them askance and whispered that perhaps they were taking it a little too far.

186

Every last one—even the women and children—became the row-diest of tavern brawlers. The law suffered greatly in their hands. They seemed determined to make up for all those centuries spent as pacifists by conducting themselves as abrasively as possible.

Which might account for their willingness when the King assigned them with the task of killing their leader. They wanted, it seemed, to prove once and for all they could be just as barbaric as the most sophisticated city dweller.

After the orders were issued, the King reclined in his throne room. He thought about all the people he would have executed in the coming months. He relished the fact that no troublesome maidens would be around to muddle it up. Yes, it was very pleasing to have everything back in order.

He tapped his fingers on the throne's arm. It was very silent in here. Where was the Oboist? Ah, yes. With Alice.

"Wait a minute!" He leaped up, thunderstruck by the thought that just entered his cluttered cranium. "I can't have Swan assassinated! I love her!"

The King dashed from his throne room.

*

"Hello, Abram," the King said to the man smoking a cigar as he hurried by.

"Evening, Your Highness. Don't go up there, you hear?" Despite this sound advice, the King barrelled on up the steep slope. "Oh well," Abram said, and returned to his cigar.

Devil's Drop possessed a particularly menacing atmosphere, to-night. The wind rattled bones of carrion long dead, and ravens flitted before the full moon, cawing portentously. Nothing was spared to make the King feel dreadfully worried.

At the top, the natives surrounded a wriggling sack and poked it with sticks. It made indignant noises at each poke. The natives jeered, struggling to inject their laughter with as much cruelty as possible.

"Ha, ha!" one native said.

"We're so jaded!" shouted a second.

"Yeah!" said a third, with forced enthusiasm. "We'll do anything to get a rush!"

The King crept up behind them and said, "Even murder the woman who nourished you for decades?"

The natives turned, faltering.

"Of course!" the first native finally retorted. "Of course we're going to murder her! That's only to begin with! After that we're going to…to…"

"Do something *really* nasty!" another finished for him, and the natives raised a half-hearted cheer.

The King sensed he was somehow to blame for their behaviour. He tried again. "Well, I'm the one who ordered you to do it. And now I'm ordering you not to. You'll still be paid in full."

The natives scoffed collectively. "Do you really think we do it for the money?" They all shook their heads at his ignorance. "We're in it for the thrill!"

"Does anyone have any beer?" asked the first native to have spoken. "I love beer!"

Suddenly, the squirming sack burst open. Swan struggled to her feet, glaring at her assailants. The natives nervously retreated a few feet. The King took this opportunity to rush past them and join Swan.

"Wait a second! There's a lot more of us than them!"

"That's right! Push them over the edge!"

"We're so bad!"

The swarm of natives inched forward, edging the King and Swan toward the forbidding cliff.

"Wait!" the King shouted. "Why are you doing this?"

"Because we're tired of life!" They advanced another step.

"Life isn't so bad!" the King said. "Have you sampled everything life has to offer?"

"Oh, yes," a native assured him. "We've tried *everything*. Twice!"

The King's boots reached the edge. Rocks skittered over the Drop. The King looked down. He couldn't see the bottom.

"What about polo?" he said.

The natives stopped. "Polo? What's polo?"

"Only the greatest sport known to man!"

"Oh, a sport?" a native repeated. "We tried sports. They're *boring!*"

The throng pressed even closer. Swan and the King were going to die.

188

"It has horses!" the King squeaked.

A silence settled over the proceedings.

"Horses don't play sports," one native said, as though stating a self-evident fact.

"*Oh yes they do!*" the King shot back. "They play *polo!* Do you want to know why?"

"Not particularly!" said the native, but the others shushed him.

"Because they know it's the only sport worth playing!"

The natives whispered among themselves. "Tell us more," one of them said finally.

"I'll quote something I read on a stone tablet once, shall I?"

"Yes!" the natives shouted, feeling back in control. "You shall!"

"It said, 'Let other men play at other things. The King of Games is still the Game of Kings!'"

The natives murmured appreciatively.

"In polo, you ride horses and whack balls with mallets."

"Ooh!" a native said. "I like whacking things!"

"Will you teach us how to play?" they asked him.

"I'll do better than that! I'll christen a league in your name. You can be the forefathers of the Kingdom's first polo league."

The natives buzzed excitedly.

"But I guess there's no need to point out that in order to commission a polo league, it is required that I am alive."

"No need at all," the natives agreed. "We'll just push Swan over, and we'll get right to it!"

"I won't be able to do it alone!" the King said hastily. "I'll need someone to bounce ideas off of. Someone like, say…Swan!"

The natives all nodded in accord. "Obviously," one said. Slowly they began to depart, murmuring excitedly. A few thanked the King before starting down the slope. Eventually, the King was left alone on Devil's Drop with Swan.

"I just saved your life," he pointed out tactfully.

"Yes," Swan replied. "Right after you endangered it. I'm leaving." She stormed away.

The King sighed. "I suppose that was to be expected."

*

The King founded the natives' polo league the very next morning, and for the following weeks he filled the void in his life by raising awareness, scheduling tournaments and appearing at games.

Eventually the league became self-sustaining, however, and he gave up the charade. For a while he busied himself with ordering his staff around, and being generally unpleasant. He commissioned enormous banquets, sending his cooks into a flurry of preparation, and at the last minute declared them cancelled due to the new diet he'd begun.

Sometimes he stood in front of the mirror and delivered long-winded decrees. He chastised his reflection for failing to be a loyal subject: it constantly stared back at him with eyes devoid of hope.

Finally he gave up that charade too, and he resigned his Kingship. He instructed his shocked messengers to announce it in the streets. When everything was arranged, he left the castle.

It promptly began to rain.

He strode dejectedly up Shepherd's Hill, and lay facedown when he reached the summit. His name would be Mud again. He was lying in mud. He breathed mud. Mud seeped between his armpits. He *was* mud.

"Mind if I join you?" said a soft voice.

Mud squelched in confusion. He was no longer a person who spoke. He was a puddle of mud that squelched.

Someone lay down beside him and also began to squelch. Mud was relieved. Squelching, he could understand. He squelched a welcome.

"What's wrong with you?" the newcomer squelched.

"I no longer have any reason to live," Mud squelched back.

"Since when?"

"A couple weeks ago. That's when my love left me."

His new friend seemed to consider this. "Okay, but what reason did you have to live before you fell in love?"

Mud pondered this a while. Finally he squelched, "None, I suppose."

"Well," his new friend squelched back, "what's the difference between then and now? Why did you go on living then?"

"It just seemed like the thing to do."

"But not now?"

"No, not really. It's not the same."

Some time passed, and Mud wondered if his new friend had evaporated.

But at last: "Why did your love desert you?"

Mud squelched a sigh. "Because I ordered her dead."

"That wasn't very nice."

"I didn't mean to. I just didn't know what I wanted."

"Well, you can't order your partner dead every time you have a moment of indecision."

"I know. I'm not a very good person." Mud paused. "Puddle of mud," he amended. He could feel his humanity creeping invasively back.

"Would you say you're very, very sorry for condemning your love to death?"

"Yes, I would most certainly say that. Without hesitation."

His new friend paused. "I forgive you."

Mud knew he was a human once again. He stood up. His new companion also stood up, who, as you might have guessed, was Swan.

They embraced.

*

From that day forward, Mud resided on Shepherd's Hill in a modest shack he built with his own hands. He never returned to being the King. Instead, he passed that job on to Sir Forsythe, who was a much worthier candidate.

By default, Countess Francine became Queen. She had never ceased pestering Forsythe, and now it paid off lavishly.

Mud and Swan greeted each new dawn with sheer disbelief at ever having found each other. They had both grown so used to being lonely they accidentally spent the rest of their lives in perpetual appreciation of one another.

One day King Forsythe and Queen Francine hiked up Shepherd's Hill, with both a gift and news for Mud and Swan. The gift was a crown for Mud, to commemorate his days as King. It was a simple affair, with golden peaks and a few gems studded around its circumference.

The news was this: in a few months, Queen Francine would have a baby. They had already decided on its name.

They would name it the King.

THE END.

Epilogue

9 years later

Mud groaned. Something was digging into his side. The ditch in which he lay was extremely uncomfortable.

He managed to fish his pocket flask from his robe. He took a swig.

"You know," he said, to no one in particular, "I think that girl really messed me up."

He took another prolonged draught from his pocket flask.

"What girl?" someone said.

Mud looked up, careful not to move too quickly. He ached all over.

Frederick stood over him, with Alice hanging from his arm. The Oboist raised his eyebrows.

"That girl," said Mud, pointing at the wagon, now a mile distant, which was hurtling away from them at a frightening speed. It was driven by a young girl who kept shooting panicked glances backward. "She knocked me into this ditch."

"Who is she?"

Mud managed to shrug.

Frederick helped him up and into a wagon that sat nearby. In the back, Frederick's gaggle of children squirmed impatiently. There were seven, and every one of them hated Mud.

The Oboist cracked his whip, and they began trundling toward Shepherd's Hill. The children, who were all musicians, began playing the narrative ballad they were working on. It was about Mud's nose, and its remarkable size. Mud glared at them.

Frederick, ever multitasking, managed to drive, kiss Alice and praise his children at the same time.

Mud didn't have children, but not for lack of trying. He and Swan had wanted a baby for years. The gods had allowed Mud to find his soul mate, but apparently they were uncomfortable with the idea of him procreating.

In nine years, Mud knew the Kingdom had changed. Perhaps it was the paved, well-kept roads. Perhaps it was the new sanitation system—with the addition of ditches shortly after King Forsythe's coronation, things began to smell a whole lot better.

But mostly, Mud thought, it was the smiling peasant faces that graced the marketplace. It was a kind word exchanged over reasonably priced goods. It was shared and widespread happiness.

He also knew these changes reflected his own kingly incompetence. He smiled to himself. Somehow, he didn't give a midden heap.

They arrived at Shepherd's Hill, and Frederick helped him hobble into his hovel and ease into his cot. The kids gave a final, resounding rendition, and the wagon trundled off again.

Swan wasn't home, and so Mud had no one to talk with as he stared at the low ceiling of his humble cottage.

He rarely enjoyed grandiose feasts anymore, and he never entertained important members of the nobility. For nine years, it seemed he had lived the same day over, again and again.

Mud noticed a crack in the boards above him, and knew he would have to mend it.

He waited for Swan to return.

Acknowledgments

Thank you to my family, for believing in me and supporting me always.

Thank you to my girlfriend, Raven, for being a loyal reader, and for being way more confident in my success than I am.

Thank you to Lucinda Austin, Matthew Daniels and Courtney Fowler, who made tremendous editorial contributions.

Thank you to the Under the Bed Writing Group, which, at the time of my joining, consisted of Alison Dyer, Denise Flint, Kelly-Anne Meadus, Sandy Newton and Kathleen Winter. I was only present for the last few meetings, but the feedback I received was invaluable.

Thank you to the users of Authonomy.com who provided feedback. They include but aren't limited to Andrew Collison, Elaina J. Davidson, Hannah Davis, Sheryl Dunn, Shoshanna Einfeld, Elinor Evans, Kimberly Gadette, Kate Kasserman, Rob K, Elizabeth Lindberg, Elizabeth Maitreyi, Joseph Miller, Annabelle Page, Duane Simolke, Victoria Tweed and Keef Williamson.

Thank you to Don McKay and Lisa Moore, whose knowledge of the craft benefited me greatly during their time as Writers in Residence at Memorial University of Newfoundland.

Thank you to the Writers' Alliance of Newfoundland and Labrador, for offering a wide array of excellent resources for Newfoundland writers.

Thank you to my cousin, Gillian Chiasson, for reading the manuscript in its early stages and for being very supportive.

Thank you to Susan Jarvis, not only for being an awesome artist but also for being awesome to work with.

Thank you to Terry Smith, who helped me alter the cover design during the final stages, and on very short notice.

Thank you to Jonathan Abbott, Lynette Adams, Bill Allan, Zack Andrews, Michael Arbou, Amanda Ash, Alyssa Ashley, Victoria Ashley, Katherine Atkins-Branigan, Beth Ann Austin, Kim Bailey, Laura Bailey, Samantha Bailey, Matt Baird, William Baird, Chris Baldwin, Paula Baldwin, Jordan Barbour, Leah Barbour, Joshua Barnes, Nathan Barnes, Susie Barnes, Celina Barry, Elizabeth Barry,

Natasha Barry, David Bartlett, Geoff Bartlett, Melanie Batten, Melissa Batten, Katherine Bawol, Ron Bearns, Matty Bee, Chelsea Beehan, Cassandra Bennett, Jessica Bennett, Joshua Berman, Ashlyn Biggin, Ashley Blackmore, Stephen Blackwood, Jon Bleakney, Ryan Bonar, Erica Boutilier, Scott Bradley, Alissandra Bragg, Robert Breen, Jessica Broderick, Christopher Bruce, Cory Buffett, Stephen Burt, Amanda Burton, Corrina Butler, Genelle Butler, Holly Butler, Katrina Butler, Justine Byrne, Adena Cahill, Amanda Calnen, Kaitlyn Campbell, Paul Campbell, Rebalee Carew, Cindi Carnell, Carla Chiasson Carpenter, Sammy Chamberlaine, Robert Chaytor, Brandon Chiasson, Denise Chiasson, Carla Chiasson Carpenter, Jennifer Codner, Emily Cole, Geraldine Coleman, Jerry Collins, Michael Collins, Colleen Connors, Bryan Conway, Sarah Cook, Lezlee Coombs, Colin Corcoran, Nate Corcoran, Alexander Corrigan, Melissa Crocker, Josh Curnew, Melissa D'Agostini, Bryan Davis, Sarah Davis, Angela Dawe, Lorelei Dean, Courtney Decker, Jessica Decker, Krista Decker, Jessica Deering, Rob Derochie, Erin Deveaux, Janice Dewling, Tanya Dewling, Chrissy Dicks, Victoria Dinham, Amber Dodge, Tasha Dominix, Catie Downton, Fahlon Drake, Katie Dray, Stephen Driscoll, Devin Drover, Catherine Ducey, Brad Dunne, Christopher Dwyer, Jen Dyke, Elizabaeth Eddy, Victoria Elliott, Victoria Elms, Katie Esty, Andrea Evanoff-Winter, Lacey Evans, Laura Fagan, Todd Felix, Melissa Fiander, Trevor Finney, Cheryl Fitzgerald, Becky Fleming, Paul Fortin, Sawyer Foster, Paul Fowler, Stephanie Fowler, Lionel Fraser, Greg Gale, Laura Genge, Erika Gill, Valerie Gillam, Gertrude Gladney, Jennifer Gladney, Kenny Gladney, Marie Gladney, Rick Glynn, Janice Godin, Angeline Goldsworthy, Sarah Gorner, Adam Gosse, Darryl Gosse, Jason Gosse, Laurie Gosse, Michele Gladney Gosse, Greg Goulet, Tyler Gracie, Alicia Grandy, Robin Grant, Linda Greeley, Ruth Hall, Richelle Hanlon, Emily Hann, Nichole Hayley, Melissa Hayter, Roger Hayter, Tammy Hayter, Terri-Lynn Hayter, Thomas Hayward, Olivia Heaney, Toni Hibbs, David Hickey, Justin Hickey, Jesse Hicks, Leslie Higdon, Robyn Hillier, Alyssa Hodder, Hudson Hogarth, Renee Hogarth, Tracey Hogarth, Victoria Hogarth, Kyle Hollett, Travis Hopkins, Megan Hoskins, Chenoa Houlihan, Mark Houlihan, Karen Howse, Scott Humphries, Tommy Humphries, Petter Hurich, Samatha Jade, Wayne Picco, Adam Janes, Jolon Jenneaux, Corey

Jones, Pat Joyce, Darryl Kean, Jordan Kean, Maria Kearney, Vinnie Keeping, Krystal Kelsey, Katelyn Kendall, Melissa Kennedy, Sarah Khraishi, Andrew King, Stephen Kitchen, Joseph Kwan, Matthew Lawlor, Doug Letto, Elling Lien, Sherry Locke, Robert Lockyer, Claudia Long, Melissa Long, Alicia Loomes, Ryan MacDonald, Kyna MacInnis, Marie MacIntosh, Leah MacQueen, Muffy MacLean, Brianne MacNeil, Ian MacNeil, Mike MacNeil, Stella Magalios, Linda Mahon, Victoria Mallard, Ashley Mancini, Imelda Manning, Jessica Manning, Kelly Manning, Kurtis Manning, Laura March, Melinda Martin, Vanessa Martin, John Matchim, Erin Maxwell, Laura Mccarthy, Krystle McConnell, Matthew Mcgean, Curtis Meeker, Kerri-lynn Melvin, Maggie Meyer, Sarah McHugh, Caitlin Mills, Sam Molloy, Tim Morris, Wendy Morris, Jason Mosher, Alex Mugford, Vicky Mullaley, Erin Murphy, Joanne Murphy, Matthew Murphy, Stephen Murphy, Kelly Myers, Vanessa Myers, Joey Neary, Chris Negrijn, Gary Newhook, Sarah Newhook, Wanda Nolan, Stephanie Norman, Nikki Northcott, Bailey Oake, Robyn Oickle, Barb Oliver, Alexandria O'Neill, Cayla O'Neill, Diane O'Rielly, Erin O'Rielly, David Owens, Megan Page, Joesie Palmer, Mathew Parnell, Desiree Parsons, Laura Parsons, Tamara Parsons, Angela Peach, Joanna Pearce, Brad Peddigrew, Adam Pennell, Melissa Penney, Tiffany Penney, Linda Pike, Candice Pinsent, Evan Power, Ross Purves, Robin Pyke, Brittany Quilty, Heather Quinlan, Krista R, Shane Randell, Natasha Simoes Re, Amanda Singleton, Kyle Rees, Simon Rees, Cathy Renouf, Chris Rex, Stephen Rhodenizer, Keagan Richer, Vanessa-leigh Rideout, Kati Rowe, Kate Rowsell, Chris Roy, Erica Roy, Jean Marie Roy, Tim Rusted, Leslie Ann Ryan, Natalie Skocyzlas, Sarah Seymour, Colleen Shapter, Barbara Sheppard, Bryanne Sheppard, Jen Sheppard, Shirley Skinner-Squires, Diedre Smith, Stephanie Smith, Jody Spurrell, Jill Squires, Renea Squires, Kaitlin Stapleton, Carolyn Stevens, Jeremy Stewart, Melanie Stewart, Robert Stockley, Stephanie Stoyles, Manda Sullivan, Steve Tapp, Hassam Tariq, Holly Taylor, Tanya Taylor, Steven Thomas, Jamal Tinkov, Stephen Tizzard, Allison Tobin, Katie Tobin, Richard Tobin, Stephen Traverse, Danielle Tucker, Deanne Tucker, Melissa Tucker, Sarah Tucker, Melissa Tulk, Leslie Vryenhoek, Vanessa Wade, RN Wagner, Aimee Wall, Taylor Wall, Danielle Walsh, Nicole Walsh, Roland Walsh, Samantha Walsh, Nikita Walters, Becca Wells, Penny

Weston, Philip Whalen, Edward Whelan, Justin Whelan, Aaron White, Courtney White, Curtis White, John White, Sarah White, Zaren White, Kayla Whittle, Sarah Whyte, Michael Williams, Michael Winsor, Rodney Woodford, Ron Woodman, Wayne Wright and Matt Van Zutphen for your support.

About the Author

Scott Bartlett was born in 1987, and has lived most of his life in Newfoundland, Canada. He began writing fiction when he was fifteen, the year he wrote the first two chapters of a novel and got distracted halfway through Chapter Three.

In high school he succeeded in finishing a book, but quickly realized it was awful and decided to never let anyone read it.

Royal Flush is his second novel. In 2007, it won the H. R. (Bill) Percy Prize.

In between novels, Scott wrote several short stories. And recently, he completed a third novel, the writing of which was funded by the Newfoundland and Labrador Arts Council. But that's another story.

Scott maintains a blog, too, where he writes about environmental issues and occasionally posts fiction: http://www.batshite.com

Photo by Karla Kenny (http://www.karlakenny.tumblr.com/)

CPSIA information can be obtained at www.ICGtesting.com
Printed in the USA
LVOW120434110112

263247LV00001B/5/P